The Endless Night

Duchess MacKinnon

This book is
dedicated to
Ralph Lamar Hester
10/08/1932-3/3/2004

He served his
country, was always
there for his family,
and was the most
amazing storyteller
ever. He was one of
the best Dad's ever.
Forever he will be
missed but never
will he be forgotten.

Acknowledgements

They say to raise a child it takes a village. The saying is no less true when publishing a book. With that being said, I have a tremendous amount of thanks that needs to be owed to those who have assisted and helped me through this entire process.

Leona Hester – Besides being my mother she gets special kudos because of her unwavering support in this process.

Angel DeFreitas - I met him because he was auditioning for the role of Jared for my videos. He has lent his image to Jared and did a phenomenal job at interpreting the character. What I had not intended was for him to become one of my best friends in the process. A huge thanks to all he has done that is book related. It's been a true honor working with him on this project and I am doubly honored by his friendship.

Kim Snider - An amazing model who is beautiful both on the outside and on the inside who kindly has allowed herself to be photographed and placed on the cover of my book. The photo's came out stunning and was exactly how I envisioned the cover.

Doug Hicks - Who helped me design the cover design. I took the photo of Kim myself, he edited the photo and created the cover. He has been a longtime friend for many years. He is also a fantastic photographer in his own right.

Mairi Campbell – Much thanks to my last minute editor who was truly a task master. She is also a brilliant author in her own right. Her website is www.mairi-campbell.com.

David Superville - For the video editing of my Jared videos. He took on a task that was almost beyond help and did a fabulous job with them. If there is a next time, I promise, I will have you do the filming.

Chapter 1

This was one of the worst crime scenes I had ever seen. Not because it was gruesome. I had already seen the ones that would make a lesser person hurl. This one was chilling in the execution. The victims were perfect in every way. Their nails were perfectly manicured. Not a hair was out of place. They wore matching black outfits. There wasn't even a smudge in their matching dark red lipstick. It was the popular color called Vampyre Kiss. Something I wouldn't have known, but one of the female officers had recognized it.

For all intents and purposes, the victims looked like they had gotten up, gone to the salon, gotten dressed, laid down side by side, and simply died. Even their hands were folded over their chests with a single red rose. It was chilling in the details.

Unfortunately, they did not die of natural causes. The medical examiner had determined on the spot that they died from a vampire attack. There were at the appropriate places bite marks and they died from loss of blood. A vampire bite after the fact does not look like what is depicted in cartoons and films with two neat puncture marks. It looks like an overzealous hickey with teeth imprints that can be measured.

They had dreamy smiles on their face as if they had been entranced. The room of a crime scene is usually completely filled with cops taking pictures and examining everything that could be evidence. However for the moment it was empty with the exception of the lead investigator, Detective Mike Anderson, and me.

This was the first time I had ever worked with him. Hell this was my first official night in Charlotte, North Carolina. I got the call to see where I was when I was just west of a town called Asheville. I hadn't even had a chance to see if my stuff for the house I was renting had arrived or if I would need to check into a hotel for the night.

I was concentrating so hard on the victims that they seemed to have little black dots floating around them and I realized the dots and tight feeling in my chest were from me holding my breath for just a little too long. "Cassandra?" I heard the voice repeat over again with increasing urgency. I realized that I was also tuning everything out including the detective.

"Sorry," I muttered.

"Do you usually concentrate this hard?" He asked with a note of concern.

"Only if it is a difficult case."

"It's not open and shut?" He asked with a hopeful look on his face. Detective Anderson was not a normal detective. He was incredibly good and he was always given the hardest cases. Unfortunately, he lacked certain social barriers, if you're being kind and if you weren't being kind, you could say he was flat out inappropriate at times. He joked a great deal and even in the short time that I knew him, he was caught whistling Jingle Bells. I could see how it would be unnerving to others when the lead detective is whistling Christmas carols while looking at a dead body. There were many complaints until his superiors had to do something with him

They couldn't just fire him because he was too good at what he did, so they did the only thing they could think of. They put him in charge of the regional preternatural unit. A position that they were having a very hard time filling. At my interview he confessed that he was just as happy to be removed from the mundane homicide investigations since they were boring.

He didn't look like a normal law enforcement officer either. He was just a little under 5 foot 9 and while not fat, he had a bit of belly that indicated that he did indulge in the stereotypical doughnut here and there. He looked like a cross between a computer lab geek and a mad scientist. He had unruly, dark, curly hair that was all over the place and thick black rimmed glasses that made his brown eyes, that were so dark you could call them black, look bigger than they were. His clothes were sloppy as if he threw on whatever was wadded up on the floor and I suspected that he had a touch of attention deficit disorder but I could be wrong there.

"Merry Christmas," I said with a smile, "there has never been a vampire in this room. Or any other magical creature. There once was a ghost but probably when this area was covered in trees and the white man hadn't even discovered America for the second time."

"So not our jurisdiction?" He looked crestfallen. I had to repress the desire to sigh and roll my eyes in exasperation. "Not necessarily. It is a very good representation of a vampire attack. Your medical examiner had every reason to believe that it was a vampire attack. It looked convincing which I think is important to investigate. It was a deliberate attempt to implicate vampires. In most places it would be successful."

"I confess I don't know as much as you do about the monsters. So for the sake of my report could you explain why it couldn't be a vampire? Besides that, you couldn't detect anything magical. The courts you know. They love their facts and what you do," he wiggled his fingers, "doesn't always convince prosecutors or judges."

I hated the finger wiggle. It wasn't annoying the first time, but when you've seen it a thousand times; you lose any sense of amusement.

"Even if no facts can be produced?"

"Exactly."

I began to think about the facts so that I could present them to him. That was the problem with magical law enforcement. Much of it was circumstantial at best and at worst pure conjecture; unlike DNA which is the ultimate smoking gun. Most of what was known about the preternatural community was based in legends and myths. The problem was that legends and myths were just that. Now it was a good idea to take them seriously in this day. Especially the multi-cultural ones. Every culture had their own form of vampire and shape shifter for instance. Egyptian hieroglyphs depicted humans in partial animal form. They even built statues, the most famous being the Sphinx.

However, for every legend, there are misconceptions. Misconceptions that could mean your life if you took them literally. One instance is that vampires were afraid of crucifixes. Myth! The Vampire King of Chicago wore one around his neck just to make a point. The same with garlic and in some cases sunlight is inaccurate, as the Vampire King of Charlotte has been known to walk in the day. Some legends had vampires being able to change into other animals. If Dracula had existed and not been a fictional character, he would not have been able to turn into a bat, mist, rat, or anything else.

So unfortunately Virginia, there is no Santa Clause that we know of. However, there are vampires, were-animals, zombies, and all sorts of things that go bump in the night. And the boogie monster that you think might be hiding under your bed? Well I wouldn't rule it out either. All because he has not come out from under the bed so to speak and made a public declaration does not mean he doesn't exist.

It was only in 1982 when the vampires came out of the coffin. Unfortunately, nobody believed it was real. The 1980's were so crazy it was thought to be a fad like the big hair and wild clothes.

After the vampires came out, one group after another started to come out of the woodwork and the skeptics started to pay attention. But the real attention didn't come into play until preternatural crimes began to occur. Crimes that could not fit any normal explanation. To be safe the courts and lawmakers ruled that any monster found was to be subjected to a swift execution. Providing the potential executor didn't turn up dead, an occurrence that happened very frequently.

After two decades of persecution the monsters were ruled as citizens providing they didn't take unfair advantage by using mind games. The economy had gone to hell in a hand basket and the essentials were that the government needed the monsters. Monsters were big business. Especially vampires, since they had been romanticized in pop culture. It saved the economy though the anti-monster groups have questioned at what cost.

Still after decades of mostly denial, but just in case we'll kill you on sight policies, there was a shocking amount of ignorance. To be fair most of it was because the monsters simply weren't willing to talk about themselves and really, could you blame them? The only thing that has been clear is that silver is deadly to most everything. For a time after that discovery, silver became more valuable than gold. Then scientists managed to make an effective synthetic silver and liquid silver nitrate. Both were proven to be effective though I didn't trust it completely.

I finally spoke, "By the size of the bite marks, it appears that the same being bit both women. However, a single vampire is unable to drink a human dry. Nevertheless two people. Their stomachs wouldn't be able to contain it all. To give you a scientific test, drink a quart of water and see how full you are. Then double that. A human being could survive 2 pints being removed. They might be weak and run down. They might even feint but a healthy one could survive. I don't know what killed these women but I do know that it was not something of the preternatural community. Another fact is that there was no struggle. In order for there not to be a struggle they would have had to be completely bespelled. Which would indicate an older vampire, at least half a century old. The older the vampire, the less blood they need to make a meal."

I realized that I was being tested and that he knew some of the facts but the last one surprised him. "Why is that?"

I shrugged, "It just is. According to interviews, Jared the local vampire king doesn't need much and he doesn't even drink pure human blood anymore. He harvests from his were-animals. Ultimately, the only vampires that really drink a lot of blood are the newbie's."

And it was the truth. If the vampires were such raving monsters they would never have been able to hide so efficiently for so long. Were they dangerous? Absolutely. The problem with being powerful and ancient was that age could corrupt. It didn't with some but many had developed godlike personas that had been repressed after being in hiding for so long. Some literally had been worshipped as Gods. Now that they were out again and at least in the USA could be themselves openly, those personas peeked out with increasing frequency.

"Do you need me any further? Or would you like to test me some more?"

"My apologies, I didn't mean to come off sounding as if I was testing you. There have been many rumors about you and I did want to see how you handled yourself when being made to defend your findings without your gift. After all there will be times you will need to testify."

"No problems." Though I silently thought that was the biggest line of bullshit I had ever heard. He knew damn well that I was good on the stand because there were transcripts of me.

"Get some rest, Ms. James. I imagine you will need it."

"Please, call me Cassandra. Ms. James makes me feel old."

"Get some rest then, Cassandra."

Chapter 2

As I got into my car and plugged in my address to the GPS I couldn't help but think about my new home. I was renting again but getting three times the place for half of what I was paying before yet making twice as much money than I was in Chicago. It was a stand alone home and not an apartment so I wouldn't have people crammed on all sides of me. I even had a yard. I wasn't sure what I would do with it, but it was all mine. For me it felt like I was on top of the world in luxury. For the first time in my life, my wretched gift was being a real profit to me.

My abilities and knowledge of the monsters was such that it cost me dearly. It cost me my family and made me an outcast to some extent because I must be a monster to know so much more than others. I remembered as a small girl I was beaten severely by my father when they were actually talking about Jared himself and I made a comment that he wasn't a monster he was special.

My name is Cassandra James and I would act as a consultant for the preternatural crimes unit and head up the preternatural studies department at Central Piedmont Community College here in Charlotte. At first there was talk that I would go to Raleigh but it was later deemed to be best to have a preternatural expert in the lair of the vampire king of Charlotte who was also the spokesperson of the council in North America and had a seat on the European Council as well.

Preternatural Studies was to be a brand new field of study but one that was necessary now. I only had 20 students this semester and like some nursing programs, the number would be capped at 20 each year. The hope is that eventually this would become a university course of study. After graduation these students would be able to consult. Whether they have any psychic skills, I don't know. But at the very least they will be able to determine when they need someone specialized and can use a level of logic to keep the police from falling down rabbit holes or getting into the habit of making all bad crimes the blame of the preternatural community. It was of course not sanctioned but the preternatural community was pretty good at policing itself and taking care of their own little problems. The police were very good also at being able to turn a blind eye when such things resolved themselves.

A few of my students might get additional training if they have the abilities to carry out sanctioned executions but those were difficult. I hated it when my hand was forced to take a life and it didn't matter if it was the walking dead or not. Some of the more callous executioners have a very black and white view of things. They believed that dead was dead and if it walked and talked, then it was their job to make it stop.

I was disturbed by the timing of an attempt to frame vampires and that was exactly what this was meant to do. It was common knowledge that Jared MacAllistair, the vampire king of Charlotte was gearing to open his masterpiece, The Mall of Endless Night. It was a mall that was going to completely eclipse anything that was ever built. You would be able to literally live and work there. It was going to have a perpetual night time theme with glittering shops to break it up. I had seen the promotional concept plans and I was impressed.

Originally they wanted to schedule me to live in a hotel until it opened so that I could live there so that I was close at hand but it was too far away from both of my jobs. I was closer to the college but was a bit further away from the police department that housed the preternatural unit but I didn't care. I found the place that I liked and I didn't know what my experience was going to be like with this vampire king. If it came anywhere close to what I had with the vampire king of Chicago, I wanted a good distance away.

It took me over an hour to get to my home between the congestion and the stupid GPS sending me in what I swear was an unnecessary loop de loop which was not helpful. I was already directionally challenged. If I continued to get sent off the beaten path just to get home, I was never going to be able to find my place or any other place for that matter.

When I arrived there were two notes on the door. Or more specifically there was a note and what might be passing for a note. Depending on what your definition of note is. The first was from the movers which meant they had been there. It was a torn corner piece of notebook paper with a careless scribbled writing that was so bad that it took me a good five minutes to make out what it said. The paper stank of stale tobacco and had stains on it that I could only assume was food. At least I hoped it was food.

We will be back tomorrow to unpack. However, we set your bed up and unpacked the bathroom boxes and some of your clothes.

The second was the exact opposite on an envelope stamped that it was from the office of the Vampire King. I noted that it had been sealed with wax which was very old fashioned and the note inside was the opposite. It was clean parchment paper that had a nice clean fragrance to it. The handwriting was incredibly elegant and neat. Fortunately, the contents aggravated me slightly but it was inevitable I suppose. Jared had wanted to meet me before when I was interviewing for the positions, but I declined citing that it would be inappropriate. The truth was that I wanted to leave Chicago badly and didn't want to meet him just in case he was spookier in reality than the Chicago King.

Cassandra,

Welcome to my city. You must be exhausted from your travels and I would love to extend an invitation for you to dine. I am most interested in meeting such a legend. Just call the number on the letterhead. My social secretary may answer.

Sincerely,

Jared

When I opened the door, I found much to my relief rows of neatly placed boxes surrounded by nearly well placed furniture. I was impressed and had braced myself for catastrophe. My bathroom was completely set up. They must have taken notes on how I had things laid out in my old place. I didn't really need three bedrooms but I wanted it anyway. One of the bedrooms was going to be my home office.

I looked at the time and realized that it was nearly nine o'clock. I glanced over at the note written by Jared and figured I might as well meet him now and that would be one thing less than I would have to do, plus I was anxious to get the first meeting out of the way. So I dialed the number.

I expected to get a social secretary. I was not expecting to get him.

"Hello Cassandra! I wasn't sure if you were going to call."

"I just got here," I said wearily.

"Really? Weren't you supposed to be here in the early afternoon?"

"I was. I can't really give details but I was at a crime scene as soon as I got here."

"Preternatural?" His voice had a tone of urgency and I suppose he had a right to be concerned. After all he headed the entire community.

"Suspected."

"So it wasn't?"

"You're fishing and I am not really in the mood." I said flatly trying to put as much disapproval in my voice as I could. I had learned that I had better set a tone on how I meant to go on or I would be so screwed.

"My apologies. I will not mention it again. So will you accept my invitation for dinner? I can have a driver pick you up."

"As long as I am not part of the meal and the meal doesn't involve nuts as I am allergic."

"Trust me," he said silkily.

"Not very likely," I retorted and he laughed heartily over it.

"Will spaghetti and the most amazing meatballs suit?"

"That should be fine. But how would you know the meatballs are amazing?"

"My were-animals. I feed the local pack of my own animal to call and truth be told any other were-animal that wants to eat. They grumble if pizza is served every night. So my kitchen actually gets used."

"Imagine that. A vampire who's kitchen is used." I say drily. "Can we make it an hour though? I need to clean up."

"My driver will be there in an hour. His name is Jimmy. Don't dress up. Just wear whatever you are comfortable in. We're fairly casual here." This was good to know. The vampire king of Chicago demanded black tie formality for any of his events. Sometimes I thought he sadistically knew that I didn't walk well in heels and he enjoyed the idea of seeing me fall on my ass.

Then I suddenly felt nervous about the entire situation. I was about to meet Jared MacAllistair, vampire king of Charlotte, and winner of GQ's Sexiest undead five times. But more to the point I was meeting the vampire that could potentially make my life a living hell or make it easier. Either way I was profoundly grateful to be out of Chicago and I knew the feeling was mutual.

For one, I knew if I stayed that sooner or later I would get killed. The vampire king hated me and made the fact very clear. Renaldo had his fingers buried very deeply into the area of organized crime and my investigations interrupted his business. I don't really think it was so much personal but more that I was an annoying bug that he felt the need to swat. I had been forced to execute two of his top vampires and he made it very clear to me that he was, "most put out" over it. However, now that I was gone he was delighted and I no longer had to deal with crappy Chicago winters or the wind. If I never heard the words lake effect snow I would be happy. Today felt like a summer day even though it was early August and I loved it.

I hastily combed my hair and pulled it up into a pony tail, brushed my teeth, and quickly changed into a floral printed skirt and blouse. Then I carefully strapped my silver knives on.

Despite the cost, I always keep at least one or two weapons infused with real silver. I simple don't trust 100 percent either silver nitrate or the fake silver compound that was formulated. It might be effective on the newer vampires but none of the ancient ones like Jared have stepped up and volunteered themselves as guinea pigs to test either. Until I had that kind of proof, I would just stick with the stuff guaranteed to get the job done. I didn't trust the single stake in the heart either. As my grandmother said, if you take the head and the heart, they won't get back up and chase you.

I twirled in the mirror looking critically and sighed. It would have to do and I cursed my appearance. I had long red hair that had a natural wave to it but instead of having blue or green eyes to go with it, I was stuck with brown. To top it off I was barely over 5 feet in height and excessively curvy. Not fat so much. I didn't dare be fat. I had to be able to fight after all. But still…I wasn't as tickled with my presentation as I would have liked and that couldn't help but make me frown just a bit.

Chapter 3

The driver arrived not long after I had finished getting ready, in a sedate black mini-van which kind of surprised me. I had expected a limo but even so I was infinitely grateful that he hadn't sent one. I knew it would draw attention and not the most ideal way to introduce myself to the neighborhood. The driver's name was Jimmy and he quickly explained that the limo would make the neighbors wonder and that the master didn't think I wanted to announce anything to the neighbors. I had to appreciate the tact and it allowed me to ride shotgun. Maybe if I pay attention, I'd learn where things are. Not likely but there was always a certain amount of hope.

Jimmy was tall but stringy with short spikey red hair and grey eyes. He had a thin red mustache that he kept touching which told me that it must be new and he was the most freckled person I had ever seen. That was one of the things that I was grateful for. I might have red hair and a fair complexion, but at least I didn't have freckles.

He wore a black suit that he quickly confessed he didn't much care for but it was a uniform and since Jared paid for it he reckon he should wear it because he didn't want to hurt his lordship's feelings. He also pointed out his name tag so that I was sure I knew he was the right person and not an imposter. It apparently didn't occur to him that an imposter could make a name tag with a duplicate name.

Jimmy was chatty and talked about the wonderful things about Charlotte and named several places that I would like to go visit, shop at, and eat at. Then he hastily added, that once the Mall was open there would be no need to go anywhere else because "Begging your pardon ma'am," he said in a southern drawl, "The so called Mall of America don't have a candle to what we'll be opening," he said with a note of overwhelming pride.

"And when is that?" I asked for curiosity and to see if the murders were connected to the opening.

"Oh no ma'am, you won't get me there. His lordship warned me that you were notorious. Jimmy, he says, "Don't tell her everything, specially about the mall." I asked him how you were notorious but he just smiled." I couldn't help but smile inside. Notorious was I?

"His lordship is correct, Jimmy. I am a very dangerous woman," and I flashed him a smile.

I could see that he had a slightly concerned expression on his face and I chuckled. Feeling a bit guilty I changed the subject with the question, "How long have you worked for Jared?"

"I've been his personal driver for two years!" He said again with a note of pride. He went on with describing the various cars that he gets to drive for his lordship. After he ran out of cars to talk about he added, "I'm lucky, I am. His lordship could have hired anyone but he chose me." He prattled on about Jared and it was very clear that Jimmy fairly worshipped the ground Jared walked. Jimmy seemed to be fairly simple but he really seemed to know his roads in the area and the cars.

After a while I realized that Jimmy while wasn't simple, he was different and had managed to find himself a living. I am sure that Jimmy's mother fairly worshipped Jared as well because he would be an employer for Jimmy for the rest of his life and by all accounts, Jared was well known for being a very good employer. What I did know was that there wasn't an ounce of magic in Jimmy. He was 100 percent human and I wasn't expecting that.

Chapter 4

After what seemed like forever in stop and go traffic we arrived at an enormous house with old style columns but otherwise appeared to have been built not too long ago. I had to admire the combination of modern and old south.

Jared was waiting at the entrance, leaning against one of the columns looking like he had deliberately posed. His hair was even blowing gently in the light breeze and I sucked my breath in with the sheer magical presence of the entire place.

I focused on the details and being in his presence was so different than seeing him on TV and splashed across tabloids and magazines. Jared said in one interview that he was a warrior when he was made a vampire. It was believable. He was very tall at around six foot four or five. In his day he would have been a giant among men. It's been said by historians that Goliath may not have really been a giant but rather a man around six foot five or six. However with mankind being much smaller than they are today, he would have been considered a giant in his time. At five feet tall he certainly appeared to be a giant to me. He had blue eyes that changed colors depending on his mood from stormy blue to sometimes brown, and dark brown hair that wasn't quite black but close to it.

He opened the door and put his hand out to help me out and I didn't want to even touch him. "Give me a minute," I said breathlessly. He stated once that while he could not be sure, he believed he was a little over two thousand years old and I believed he was every bit of that.

"Are you okay?"

"I will be. I just need to get my bearings." I closed my eyes so as not to be disturbed by him and began to concentrate on my shields, visualizing each one so that I didn't feel like I was drowning in a vortex of magic.

I opened my eyes to test the shields and smiled. "There, all better." He smiled back and if I hadn't been sitting, I swear I would have gone weak at the knees. I wanted to blush and stammer like a teenage girl. Seriously, a man should not be this good looking.

"Excellent. I trust Jimmy did a good job?"

"He was wonderful." I said enthusiastically because really he was.

Jimmy then interrupted enthusiastically, "She was a very good passenger, my lord. But you are right. She is notorious even though I still don't know what that word means. I guess it means she asked when the Mall of Endless Night is to open but I told her that was a secret and she didn't press for any more details."

"Very good, Jimmy," Jared said with a smile. "Petunia just had her kittens and won't let anyone get near her. She might allow you though. She elected to have them in the barn."

Jimmy saluted and began running off to what I presumed was the barn. "I wonder when he's going to realize that he forgot to park the car." Jared said wryly.

"Probably sometime shortly after Petunia scratches him for interfering with her mothering."

"No, Petunia loves him. The weirdest cat ever. She hates all of us of course. She knows naturally what we all are and considers us dangerous. However, Jimmy is different. He rescued her a few months ago in a storm that came through here and she's been attached to him since. The Barn is where all the cars and whatnot are stored. He's very good at taking care of them and the former caretaker was ready to retire. He has an apartment of his own attached to the barn. He eats at the house sometimes. The rest his mother visits. Now, may I escort you in?" He held his arm out and I took a deep breath and placed my hand gently on his arm.

"You're smaller than I thought you know. By Renaldo's account you're larger than life."

My mouth couldn't help but tighten at Renaldo being brought up.

"He doesn't much like me."

"No, he really doesn't. He was profoundly grateful that you decided to move off to me and wished me much joy of you. Is it true you killed two of his top vampires?"

"Legally executed and yes I did. But they deserved it and it was a sanctioned hunt."

"Johann and Jeremiah were fairly powerful vampires."

"I didn't say it was easy."

He laughed and I realized that he was more dangerous than Renaldo ever would be. He was charming and his charm seemed to affect me and I really didn't like that.

However, I allowed him to escort me into the house and I am sure even Emily Post would be pleased with my manners in handling the situation.

Chapter 5

When I crossed the threshold I realized that much of the energy was contained in the place. I took a deep breath and said, "Wow!"

"Wow?" He queried looking intently.

"There is quite a bit of energy contained in this place."

"Ah. I knew you were sensitive but not this sensitive or I would have made dinner arrangements elsewhere and if you want I can still."

"No, I will be fine. I was merely commenting. There's a lot of energy for a place this size. If it was a massive structure like the hotel that Renaldo has I would have expected it. I'll be fine." Shit I was babbling.

"I have most of the cities were-leopard popular stopping by here at least once a week if not more. And there are the vampires visiting. All done in shifts unfortunately. We're rarely together at once time but that will change when the Endless Night opens. If you can wait half an hour, we can all sit down for the next shift."

"How homey and I can wait," I said. I realized that I sounded a little derisive and that really wasn't my intent. I wasn't trying to mock and I felt myself blush slightly.

"Yes," Jared said simply. "Though family-like is a better description. My leopards are to some extent my family. I gain power from my own animal to call so it really is in my best interest to keep all my people healthy and happy."

"In my family, we ate together only on special occasions."

"How sad. While I cannot join them for the meals, I enjoy being present for at least one of the shifts so that I can keep up with their lives. Allow me to show you some of the house."

I agreed and naturally I was impressed with it all. It was a contrast of elegant old world sophistication and modern amenities. One issue with some of the older vampires has been their ability to adapt to the rapid changes that of this age. Jared seems to have not suffered the problems that some had.

When I asked about it, he looked at me gravely.

"I've noticed one thing about mankind. We don't seem to want to embrace change and often fear it. I've never been one of those who feared change. I've seen what modern medicine has done for instance. For example inoculation. I've watched small pox wipe out whole villages. Now it is a disease that is unheard of now. How can that be bad? Instead of open sewers that carry diseases to the population we have septic systems. The world is a million times different than it was when I was human and in some ways it is worse but in many ways it is better."

We ended up in the library sitting across from each other debating the merits of modern electronics and it was a profound relief. I would never have had this conversation with Renaldo. I would not have been happy being alone in the same room as him. "I've been planning to ask if one of your vampires would be willing to come in for the class that I am teaching on vampires."

"I'll come in myself for your students to have a question and answer session if you like."

"Wouldn't you be too busy with the preparations of the Endless Night?"

"Your class is in the daytime?"

"Oh." And I blushed. I could have just died from the mortification that my class was a daytime class and he was the only vampire in the southeast to our knowledge that could walk in the daylight. For that fact alone is why I must not ever underestimate his abilities. He could only be a hundred years old and he would be more dangerous because walking in the daylight was most definitely a mark of power.

"Dinna blush fer making a wee mistake lassie." He dropped his American accent instantly to a Scottish one. "So what were you investigating earlier?" I opened my mouth to answer and shut it tightly before I could say something.

"You promised," I said sternly and I realized this was a big huge mistake. I found him distracting and when he wasn't distracting me, his entire house was with people roaming about. I stood up to leave and he put his hand on my arm. "Don't go; I'll try to behave myself." A bell rang that reminded me of a school house bell. He led me into a huge dining room with a table that could have easily sat 40.

The plates were already set and I asked, "Is there anything I can help with?" He knew that I was changing the subject.

"It's pretty well taken care of."

"Will you introduce me to your were-leopards?"

He smiled and said, "Absolutely. It will be my pleasure in fact." I was a bit fascinated and couldn't help but wonder if it was a ploy. I couldn't remember all the names because the introductions were so quick and had been interrupted by a group of about ten carrying huge bowls filled with pasta and trenchers filled with meatballs and sauce. The last one to enter came up.

"Cassandra this is Dominica and our cooking mistress here. Dominica, this is Cassandra James."

Dominica was a graceful woman with black hair pulled up into a tight bun with olive colored skin and merry black eyes that had a slightly exotic slant to them. "The Cassandra James?"

"I suppose so."

"We've heard a lot about you."

"All good I hope," I said lightly not sure what they had heard about me.

"A little good, a little bad. You are very well respected though."

The rest that had trooped in were whispering and looking at me with a mixture of concern and curiosity."

The smell of the food was such that I couldn't help but help my plate and begin eating. The meatballs truly were the best I had ever tasted. "These are masterpieces," as I reached for my second helping.

"Thank you," Dominica replied who was sitting across from me. "My grandmother was Italian and she taught me how to cook. Unfortunately, she didn't know how to cook anything that was not Italian." It was nice and if Jared wanted to pull my guard down he had done a masterful job at it. It was like a large family with some bickering, talking, laughter, and familiarity. Jared sat at the head of the table looking onward with his face somewhat hard to read.

When I set my fork down, Jared stood up and asked if I wanted to walk in the gardens out back before I had to go and maybe it wasn't very wise of me but I accepted. The garden was small but smelled sweetly. In the distance you could see lightening bugs flash their lights. He talked about the variety of what was planted and we ended up just sitting in the darkness without saying anything.

Seriously, I finally asked, "When is the mall opening?"

"What were you investigating?"

"No fair."

"Very fair, Cassandra. I suggest the exchange of information since you seem to be interested in it and I can't help but wonder if what you were investigating early isn't tied somehow."

"Fine," I grumbled figuring that it wasn't going to really compromise anything since I knew he had nothing to do with it. "But you go first."

"I intend on opening the mall either after Christmas or just after the New Year. However, I and a fair portion of my leopards and vampires will be moving in a week. Two at most."

"How guarded is the information?"

"Pretty guarded. Most of the leopards and vampires that will be coming are unaware of it. Your turn." I sighed. I wasn't sure if I should be sharing this information but I decided to because it couldn't really hurt anything. I was sure he wasn't behind it.

"I saw two bodies today. Both identical in how they died and in general how they looked. By all intents and purposes they appeared to have died from a vampire attack. Yet I know for a fact that was not possible since no vampire had ever touched them or been in the room they were found in."

"How good was it?"

"Very good. The medical examiner had already declared it a vampire homicide. Only I could prove otherwise. Mostly because the bite marks were the same and as you are aware, a single vampire couldn't drink that much blood."

"Thank you for warning me that something might be up that I need to keep an eye out on." Shit.

"Stay out of the investigation." I warned. He smiled the smile he used to get him on GQ and any other magazine that wanted to give him sexiest undead.

"For you, I will keep my nose out of it."

"For me?"

"Yes. For you."

"Why?" I queried and I felt my heartbeat speed up because I realized that we were totally alone.

"You're actually trustworthy. You don't hate us with a passion. You actually care about justice and have made an effort to learn about us. One day I would love to know how you gained so much information."

"I can answer that for you. It was my grandmother."

"Your grandmother?"

"She knew about you all before you ever went public. She said it was knowledge that was handed down through the generations of the family. She knew about vampires, were-animals, and other creatures that have not come public. She taught me all that she knew."

"That's dangerous information."

"She's dead so nobody will come after her."

"You have a great deal of respect. Even Renaldo who hates you has a certain amount of respect for you and that is hard to come by from him."

I was impressed. I had no idea about Renaldo and in his world respect was everything.

"It's getting late and I expect my movers will be there at the crack of dawn in the morning."

"Jimmy didn't come to supper which means he is totally engrossed with Petunia right now and the kittens. It'd be a shame to make him leave them now. I'll take you to your place myself if you would like."

An hour later I was falling asleep surrounded by my lavender scented sheets and realized that I was on dangerous territory. I actually liked this preternatural community. I didn't much care for Chicago. The vampire king was a male chauvinistic prick and had his hand in so much underground crime that he made my life hell. He had a total disregard to his people and if his actions set someone up for execution, well he enjoyed the fact that it tormented me to be the one who got to do it. I think he secretly hoped that I would be killed but each execution made him more frightened of me. He saw me as the one who could potentially execute him if he made a mistake. And yet he apparently respected me. That fact probably explained why I was still alive.

I tried not to dwell on the fact that Jared escorted me to the door and lifted my hand up to his lips and while I couldn't swear since I had never had my hand kissed before, he lingered just a little too long with kissing my hand and his parting words. "Cassandra?"

"Yes?" I whispered breathlessly because he still had my hand."

"Welcome to my city." And he was gone.

Chapter 6

I woke up reluctantly to the sound of ringing coming from my cell phone. The movers were calling to ensure they could come over and finish. It took all morning and well into the afternoon but at the end of it, I saw my place in perfect order. I couldn't help but sigh in satisfaction. I hated moving but this was the most luxurious move I had ever made. I was delighted beyond words and profoundly glad that all had gone well. Especially since the note they left had not inspired a huge amount of confidence in me. Ultimately, it was most definitely money well spent.

I was waiting for the Internet installation guy to arrive and then I could leave to actually fill my fridge and cupboards. My cell phone rang and it was Detective Anderson.

"Cassandra."

"You met the vampire king." He said with a bit of accusation in his tone. The tone really took me by surprised.

"Of course. It's only polite to meet him." I couldn't help but have a defensive tone. Especially as I knew that I had done nothing wrong.

"Yes but not usually the first night in."

"Actually, it is required that you show respect and meet the leader of the community as soon as humanly possible. Events led to it being last night. Is there a problem with the timing and how do you know?"

"We keep a surveillance of the place and you were observed going in and going out. Several hours apart."

I took a deep calming breath as I had been taught to do. "Yes," I said as calmly as I could as I told myself not to lose it. "He fed me dinner! So of course it would be several hours in his company! Is that a problem?"

"Are you sure you didn't become dinner too?"

"Don't be silly, of course not," I couldn't help but snap. So much for the calming breath. "Nor did I donate to anyone else. He has his own were-leopards that are compelled to obey him which includes feeding him. I am the preternatural consultant here. How well I do my job is how well I get along with the community. I would rather like to have a good relationship with the community and not deal with a vampire king that is trying to fight me every step of the way. If that is such a problem for you, then I can always step down. You really want Jared to play nice."

I was absolutely furious over the entire situation and figured if I was in for a penny, I might as well be in for a pound and added, "The College is paying more than enough for me to live without this." Maybe it was a threat but I couldn't have cared less. I didn't want to be a consultant if I were constantly defending everything. Especially since rules of etiquette demanded that I present myself to the Vampire King as soon as possible. After a few moments of silence, Detective Anderson spoke.

"I was being an ass wasn't I?"

"Yes you were," I said unapologetically and he winced.

"I'm sorry. I didn't mean for it to sound like an attack. I'm not very good with people." He sounded sincere but I just didn't know him well enough to know if it was real or not. So I gave him the benefit of the doubt and hoped for the best.

"No worries. Just stay out of my relationships with the preternatural community. For every friend I make in the community, the safer I am and the more efficient I am. Why do you have his place under surveillance in the first place? Has he done something in the past that I need to know about?"

"Just because. If he is doing something wrong we'd like to know."

"Well that will come to an end you know. He is actually moving directly into the Mall of Endless Night."

"How do you know?"

"He told me." Detective Anderson whistled low. "Nice."

"Seriously, I'd like to stay friends with this vampire king if at all possible. He isn't lying about his age. He really is 2000 years old at least. I'd hate to have him treat me like the Chicago King did. I'm good but I'm not that good if he decides he wants to see the last of me."

"The Human Society really doesn't like him. Also we have reliable information that the Society for Humans Only has moved into the town. "

"What? That's a west coast group. What are they doing here?"

"Expansion?"

"And your reliable information is very reliable?" I was feeling a little light headed and sick in my stomach.

"My source has never been wrong. What the matter?"

"Oh my relationship with that particular organization isn't the best in the world."

And that was the understatement of the decade and might be a contender of the understatement of the century.

When the reality that vampires and other monsters existed grassroots campaigns sprung up overnight to stamp them out. It might not have been pitchforks and torches, but it was pretty awful and nearly accurate. Most definitely not one of mankind's finest moments in some instances.

Eventually the two major ones to emerge were the Human Society and the Society for Humans Only. The Human Society was primarily east of the Mississippi but had some of its power curtailed by legal battles. The Humane Society was currently fighting them on their name in the courts because they felt the name affected their fundraising abilities.

The Society for Humans Only was led by the Reverend Alexander Monroe and he was completely rabid about the monsters. He looked at it as a holy war and so did his followers. He was ruthless and without mercy. Oh, and did I fail to mention that he hated me personally with an absolute passion.

"Any details that you would care to share, Cassandra?"

"Nothing to really concern you too much now. If it becomes an issue, I'll give you more details."

"Okay," Detective Anderson said skeptically. "Could they have orchestrated something like these murders?"

"Absolutely." I said without hesitation.

"You sound very confident."

"Reverend Monroe is conducting, in his eyes and in the eyes of his followers, a holy war. It is in their opinion, their moral obligation to humanity to stamp out this evil. Don't ever underestimate the power of a fanatic. Especially fanatics that have a nearly inexhaustible amount of resources backing up that conviction."

"Maybe there won't be any more murders and we can figure out the ones we have."

"Yes, that would be very nice indeed." I thought to myself, nice, just not very likely. There was something more going on with those two women and I had a feeling that it was the start of something more.

Chapter 7

Unfortunately I was right and Detective Anderson was losing his warped sense of humor rapidly in the entire matter. In fact, things had gotten so bad that my students ended up with an impromptu assignment to write a paper describing why they chose this course of study, any skills that they have, and what they know or think they know about the preternatural community because I was busy examining my seventh corpse.

This one was a pretty asian girl with long glossy black hair. She was a high school teacher. According to her identification she was only 30 years old. When her family was told they were inconsolable. The victim before her was a male construction worker. He was tall and heavily muscled. His family was confused because they couldn't think of anyone wanting to harm him. As his mother said, "All he ever cared about was God, dog, and his truck." He was the only one that the Vampyre Kiss lipstick had not been applied on.

"Do the victims have any ties to any anti-monster organization?" I asked later at headquarters. Detective Anderson looked up from the computer where he was slowly typing out his report in a hunt and peck style.

"None that are known."

"Are you sure? This is a fairly conservative state and being a member of an anti-monster organization would almost be a rite of passage."

Conservative was such an understatement. I drove by one house and the car parked in the driveway still had a Bush/Quayle bumper sticker on the car and if you ever had an overwhelming desire to find God, just a pick a direction and you will not only find a church, you will be able to pick your denomination. I had also become convinced that you had to be a member of an anti-monster organization to be allowed to worship at some churches.

"I've triple checked, Cassandra. In fact a few of them were even sympathizers though the others were like Switzerland in neutrality. The toxicology report came back to the first victims. They were given a high dose of a sedative. They didn't feel a thing."

"Well crap!"

It's insane!" He burst out. "No pattern! Different religions! Different genders! Different social background! Even different body types! It's obvious it's a serial killer. But who, what, and why? What is making them pick the victims?"

"To keep us guessing. They know they don't want to be typed in case they are caught. The only thing that is the same is the way the victims die."

"Oh and here is something that will warm the cockles of your heart. Reverend Monroe arrived into town last night and has an important announcement to make."

I felt for an instance that time had stopped. "You're sure?" I asked as casually as possible.

"Yep, the press conference is at two."

"Awesome. This just gets better and better."

"It could be worse, Cassandra. The media is going to find out about these deaths sooner than later. When they do the shit is going to hit the fan," Detective Anderson said wearily.

"That should be interesting. I've never seen shit hit a fan before." I said lightly to alleviate some of the gloom.

Detective Anderson flashed me a quick grin. "Smartass."

"Someone has to be. Seriously, I'm rather surprised some enterprising soul with a police scanner hasn't figured it out. If this were Chicago by the second scene, the media would be all over this."

"It appears we are a little more innocent than Chicago," Detective Anderson said a bit wryly.

"Probably. Being historically linked to organized crime really does make people a little more suspicious."

"It's time you know, to bring Jared in on this," Detective Anderson said reluctantly.

"I agree. We can't really avoid it anymore. He's already annoyed because he knows something is going on and we aren't including him. Let's see how the press conference goes first though."

"Would you like me to go with you to Jared's?"

I had to admit that the weeks working with Detective Anderson had been nice. He had gotten used to me and had agreed to let me do my own thing because I had always proven true. In turn, I didn't say a single word about his various crime scene antics which were interesting to say the least. The father of one victim wanted to punch him because of his jolly seeming demeanor. It was a method of coping though and I recognized that. We had become friends which was nice since I tended to be solitary.

"No, I'll be fine."

"Suit yourself then."

Chapter 8

When the press conference started they made a show of introducing Reverend Monroe. He was greyer and has lost some weight but looked the same as I remembered. He was just shy of six feet tall with a bit of a belly overhanging. His hair was salt and pepper grey that was becoming more salt than pepper, and had a square jaw . His mouth was pinched and turned down. Sometimes I often wondered if the man ever smiled for real. It has always been my opinion that he only smiled when it was good for his show ratings. He didn't look like he'd have a deep baritone voice but he did, and while I didn't like him, I had to grudgingly admit he was a good orator. Lately his grey eyes had been framed with silver wired glasses whenever he read from notes.

They did a close up to his hand and you could see the faint scars of a bite mark. He claims he was bitten by a vampire but I knew the truth behind them. He stepped in front of the podium, adjusted his glasses, cleared his throat and began. He rarely looked down to the sheet of paper he had in front of him and maintained eye contact with the camera. Again, you might not like him, but he was a born speaker.

"I am here because I fear for the safety of the people from your vampires. They have gone rogue and instead of protecting the public the police, and most specifically your preternatural team, is covering it up. This new consultant of theirs, the famous Cassandra James, is nothing more than a monster and she has the entire team bowled under her influence. Much like she did with the team in Chicago." I snorted at that. The team in Chicago was owned by the vampire king and not me. "I wonder what she is giving to ensure that control?"

I sucked in a deep breath of outrage with the classic, imply a woman is a whore and you will be stronger because really, a woman couldn't really be good at anything except making babies.

"Demand truth and honestly from your police. They are the ones who are supposed to be protecting you. Ask them why seven murders have happened and the people of Charlotte are not even informed so that they can protect themselves! This is a gross abuse of power and it makes me wonder what side the police really are on."

He stepped down and declined to take further questions. The phones at the station began ringing off the hook.

"Holy shit," Detective Anderson said quietly.

"Yep. Holy shit indeed."

"He doesn't like you much does he?"

"Not really. We're going to have to set up our own press conference."

"I suppose we should," Detective Anderson said glumly. "This is the part of my job that I really hate."

"I'm not a big fan of it either myself."

"I'll set it up for tomorrow if that is alright with you, Cassandra."

"It is, and I will go give Jared a heads up if he doesn't know already since his community is going to be the public's only suspect."

"Are you sure you wouldn't like me to go with you?" Detective Anderson offered though he didn't seem very happy with the idea.

"No, I'll be fine. Truly."

When I got in my car, I flipped my cell and dialed the number that I had placed on the memory bank.

"Cassandra. I haven't heard from you in weeks."

"I need to come over and talk to you."

"Yes, you do. About the seven bodies? Do you need Jimmy to get you?"

"No, but I wouldn't mind the address so that my GPS can find you."

"I'll give you the address. I saw the press conference of course"

"I figured. I will discuss it with you when I get there."

I quickly plugged the location he gave me in my GPS and was off.

Chapter 9

I sighed with profound relief when I reached the house. The GPS only recalculated three times which was a record for me. Detective Anderson made fun of me at first because I used my GPS religiously. Then he rode with me and saw how directionally challenged I really was. Now his secret prayer is that there isn't a crime scene that can't be found on GPS. I parked the car in front of the columns and was greeted by a non-descript older man of medium height but with features that didn't really stand out. Except his mouth. He had the type of mouth that looked as if he had something intensely sour in his mouth.

"His lordship is waiting for you in the gym."

"What's he doing in the gym?"

"Working out I would presume." He said in a tone that was almost outright rude and if he wanted to play that game I could dish out a helping of my own.

"How interesting," I said with as much derisiveness and arrogance I could muster in my voice catching his eye. He swallowed visibly and added, "He trains his guards in sword fighting and general rules of war fare. Please allow me to escort you to him."

"Thank you," I smiled and put my hand on his arm. One point to me, zero to the arrogant butler.

He led me out the back of the house where a large building stood. I saw it the first time but didn't think much about it.

When I entered the building I was most definitely treated to a vision. Jared was stripped down to his waist. He wasn't grotesquely muscled like some body builders can be. But he was definitely proportionately muscled. He moved with a natural grace that was beautiful and he was very confident with the sword. He wasn't wearing his kilt. He was wearing something worse. Leather pants that looked like they had been painted on. You could tell that he was proportionately muscled in his legs as well though I was trying very hard not to notice.

I sat down on the side lines watching as he moved gracefully from opponent to opponent who were also very good but there was a noticeable edge that he had that was somewhat indefinable. It was hypnotic to watch. I had been practicing with sword, knives, and martial arts for years because I was more likely to have a vampire or monster come at me with ancient tools than for them to come at me with anything else. He was the best that I had ever seen. He looked every inch the Viking warrior and was proof of why they were so feared.

When he finished with his last opponent, he looked over at me and I couldn't help but notice that he was very pissed off.

"So Reverend Monroe is in town and there have been identical murders besides the two you mentioned the first day I saw you."

"Yes. I was at the seventh one this morning." He waited until everyone had left through a door before he spoke again.

"And you didn't think I might like to know about a little more about it?" He asked sarcastically.

"Not particularly," I lied and he knew I was lying.

"You should have been keeping me in the loop." He said angrily.

"Actually, as a consultant all my actions were totally appropriate. Do you honestly think I shared information with the vampire king of Chicago?!?" I said even more angrily. Probably because I actually felt a little guilty not testing the waters when it came to trusting him. Instead I painted him with the same brush as Renaldo.

"Of course you wouldn't!" He exploded. "The problem, Cassandra is I am NOT the Vampire King of Chicago! I am Jared MacAllistair, the Vampire King of Charlotte, North Carolina and I don't have my fingers in every possible form of organized crime. Dinna you understand? The days of our being able to hide from the public are over and all of us, we need to be able to co-exist in this society. The perk is that I no longer have to pretend to be something that I am not! So dammit, let me help the police because it is in my long term best interest to have a very good working relationship with law enforcement."

"Protocol says..."

"To hell with protocol, Cassandra," he shouted. "It was protocol never to disagree with the king or else you would get your head chopped off or imprisoned. Even if that king was a stupid twit that was leading the country into an unmitigated disaster. Sometimes protocols need to be judged on a case by case."

I opened my mouth to retort but he held a finger up and I hated how superior and arrogant he could be.

"Be that as it may, Cassandra. I've got a gift for the police."

"Oh?" I tried not to feel nervous but couldn't help myself. Renaldo gave little gifts to the police as well and they were not welcome ones.

"Even though you were determined to keep me unaware of the activities, I knew about what was going on. I keep 24 hour video surveillance on my properties and someone entered and left the place of the fourth victim. I am a silent partner of the company that owns that complex. The tapes are being delivered to the police department even as we speak. I didn't know until last night. If I had known I would have made sure the police would have the tapes before now."

Apparently Jared gave unwelcome gifts as well. They just weren't the ones I wanted to hear or see. However, what could I say? He at least didn't add that if he had been kept in the loop perhaps there wouldn't be victims five, six, or seven.

"Cassandra, have you ever consider in light of the press conference that this whole thing isn't about framing me and my vampires but rather aimed at you. I noted that Monroe wasn't a fan of yours." He asked it softly and I looked up and met his piercing blue eyes. I had never been mind fucked by anything, nevertheless a vampire, but I couldn't help but wonder if he might be the exception to the rule.

"Yep. He doesn't much like me."

"Why?"

"Probably because I have unusual abilities and he is an equal opportunity bigot."

Jared grunted and gave me an unconvinced look. "It sounded more than simple bigotry to me. Keep your secrets if you wish lass, but dinna mistake me as a fool. I know when something is personal and he had the look of something personal there."

I flushed a bit angrily. "I should go. I gave you the news I intended."

"News that you could have simply phoned in, Cassandra. Why show up here in person? Not that I mind your lovely company." He looked me up and down. I couldn't help but flush because the entire tone of the room had changed instantly.

Damn he was right. Why did I come? I never actively sought the company of the preternatural community before but that's what I did. Was it because I envied the seemingly family atmosphere that I missed in my own childhood? Sure my great-grandmother ended up raising me and giving me her last name. However, she wasn't exactly what you called warm. She knew what was going on at home long before it came to a head. She could have taken me out of there a dozen times. However, she did give me a new name eventually and at least encouraged me to profit from my curse.

"I don't know why I didn't just tell you all this on the phone," I said with a frustrated voice.

"Here, take the sword next to the wall."

"What?"

"Come spar with me."

"No thank you. I don't much care for humiliation and you would kick my ass all over next week."

"Maybe or maybe not. You killed Johann with a sword."

"A girl can get lucky from time to time."

"Johann wasn't sloppy to be killed from dumb luck."

"Fine. Try not to hurt me."

"Trust me," he said a little bitterly and while I didn't trust him much I knew he wouldn't deliberately hurt me. However, he was still very angry with me and there is one thing I've learned in life. If someone says to trust them, usually, it means you should do the opposite.

Chapter 10

I am not a huge fan of book burnings. I think it is censorship of the worst kind because it is an attempt to destroy a person's creative voice. With that being said, there are times when I wish Bram Stoker's Dracula would disappear off the face of the earth. It has done more damage to humanity then anyone will ever know. In fact, it could almost be used as a guide on what vampires aren't. Granted vampires, were-animals, and the like are very strong. Stronger than an average human but they aren't Superman strong.

The sword I picked up was light and well balanced. The pommel was comfortable to grip. The blade was stunning with engravings. It was a very superb sword. When I commented on the quality, Jared mere said, "Thank you. I made it a couple of decades ago. Before you start Cassandra, close your eyes for a moment and feel the energy in the room. Drop some of your shields. Don't allow blocking everything out drown out your special senses."

He was right. I felt an entire different set of awareness and when he struck the first time, I could almost feel him make the decision to make a move before he did it. The swords rang and I was meeting him blow to blow. I was barely aware that a small crowd had congregated at the edge of the gym watching with fascination and I suspect surprise. They weren't the only ones that were surprised.

His reach given his height was very wide, however, I was fast and agile which made a huge difference. My muscles were aching and I wanted desperately to try to get to a near kill shot so that I could say that I had done it. Eventually he over-extended just slightly and presented me the opportunity. It was just a subtle mistake that he immediately tried to correct, but I took advantage before he could maneuver himself out of and had him on his back with me on top.

He looked vaguely surprised and said; "very good lassie," then he smiled and completely rolled me until he was sitting on top of me. "Dinna forget that the fight doesn't end until you have my head and heart."

"No," I said breathlessly. "I'll never forget the important things when it matters." I could feel his weight on me and it was disturbingly pleasant. He reached up and brushed a stray tendril of my hair off my cheek and I almost forgot to breath. "It's a good thing we're not alone," he whispered. I heartily agreed. He got up and I realized that it wasn't just his were-animals watching. Detective Anderson was there and he was very sober looking.

"I owe you an apology Cassandra," he said. "When they brought you on, I thought you were just a practical knowledge person with some psychic skills. But if this was a real fight, you could have killed him couldn't you?"

"Perhaps. But I wouldn't put any wagers on it. I certainly don't want to put it to the test. He wasn't fighting for his life and there is an edge that he would bring into a fight to the death. His depth of psychic skills is unknown. Plus every were-leopard in this room would have been all over me too. But what are you doing here?"

"Looking for you and fortunately finding you safely. Someone broke into your home. We can only presume they were looking for you. We weren't sure if you were there and been taken so I was sent to check to see if you might be here since I knew you were coming here. You gave me quite the scare because I tried your cell but nobody answered."

"How bad of a mess did they make?"

"They set a fire. That's how we knew. A neighbor reported seeing smoke."

I felt a little faint, "And were they good arsonists?" I inquired trying to sound as casual as possible.

"Amateurs though even amateurs get lucky. There's fire damage in the kitchen but mostly it's water and smoke damage. I'm trying to get a hotel room with guards cleared for tonight. I don't believe it is coincidence that this happened so soon after that press conference."

"Shit!" I was safer in my own home than in a hotel room. Especially if someone was trying to get at me.

"Cassandra, they didn't burn the place down but the place isn't habitable. There's going to have to be repairs."

"She could stay here with me tonight," Jared volunteered.

"No," both I and the Detective said in unison.

He said no because of how it looked, I said no because I felt an attraction to the vampire king and being under the same roof was a very, very, very bad idea.

"Just for tonight so that you can get the manpower together," He said reasonably. I wanted to argue but the look on Detective Anderson's face was that of someone wanting to take the offer but not wanting to. I sighed and said "Fine. But just for tonight."

"Excellent!" Jared said. "By the way Detective Anderson, would you care to dine with us?"

Detective Anderson was totally shocked with the offer that he stammered sure looking at me closely.

"Melina, show Cassandra to the brown room."

"Wouldn't the green room be better?" a blond perky girl asked.

"No. The brown room has the best bathroom."

'The brown it is," she said happily.

Melina was one of those cheerleader type girls with blonde hair, blue eyes, and legs that were forever long. She was also incredibly cheerful. One might even use the term perky. She lead me down several corridors and up a staircase before opening the door. The brown room was a symphony of browns but enormous. The first room was more a living room space with a small office space to the side. Off the room was a large bathroom with a swimming pool like tub. The bedroom was as big as the bathroom and living room combined. She was jabbering on and on about nothing and I kind of tuned her out when out of the blue she became very serious and said, "He likes you." She said simply which startled me.

"Is that bad?" I felt distinctly uncomfortable with the turn in the conversation and she must have picked up on it.

"Absolutely not. He hasn't liked anyone in decades."

I thought back at the vampire of Chicago and he took his mistresses from his own were-animals.

"Doesn't he have at least one of you as his mistress?"

"He keeps his hands off us though a few have tried just because we would feel a little more secure if he had one of us. Not that he is a monk. He just hasn't had anyone serious."

"But he always has someone on his arm for the press."

"Well yeah. He does. But all because he has someone to escort doesn't mean he is dating them"

It was definite food for thought. I rather suspected that there was more to Jared MacAllistair than his public persona had carefully cultivated. He didn't impress me as the playboy everyone treated him as.

"Now if you don't mind, Cassandra, Detective Anderson, is he single by chance?"

I glanced at her slightly startled, and gave her an assessing look, but she seemed serious.

"As far as I know he is very single."

She smiled and said, "Good. You'll introduce me to him?"

Now wasn't that interesting. "Sure, I would love to."

I would never have thought Detective Anderson as being attractive but I guess he appeals to someone. Melina for one. She smiled and I couldn't help but smile back. Detective Anderson I had a feeling was going to have something to think about that didn't involve solving crime puzzles. I had a feeling this was going to be the challenge of his life.

Chapter 11

Dinner was the grand affair that it had been the first night I had come. Jared sat at the head of the table looking on as his cats chatted with each other and laughed. Detective Anderson was totally fascinated by this side of the vampire king and we chatted among ourselves.

I introduced Melina to Detective Anderson who looked startled by the introduction. She held her hand out for him to kiss and he wasn't sure what to do with it until I prompted him, "You're supposed to kiss her hand." He blinked owlishly and did as he was told and was had a look of confused astonishment when she blushed and giggled.

You had to feel sorry for the man just a bit since he was way out of his depth. As for Melina, she wasn't the coy innocent that she put on. When he wasn't looking at her she had a cool calculating look of someone who knew what she wanted and was going to get it. Still, Detective Anderson? He wouldn't have been anywhere near my list. For his part he had the look of a bachelor who realized suddenly that he was being hunted.

"I shouldn't stay here tonight. If I check into a hotel, I should be fine for just one night." I said firmly.

"Detective Anderson, do you have the manpower to have someone outside her hotel door tonight?" Jared asked quietly.

"Honestly, it would be a stretch to put someone in place right now."

"It's done. I have excellent security. She should stay here for tonight until you can come up with a better alternative tomorrow."

"I appreciate this feeling of all-inclusiveness" I said sarcastically.

"Sorry." Detective Anderson and Jared said in unison.

I didn't like that I couldn't decide my own fate or that I didn't seem to have the right to change my mind. However, it was just one night. I anxiously wanted my own things back though. I felt like stamping my feet to some extent and scream, "I want my lavender scented sheets back so that I could sleep."

I realized that Jared was looking at my face intently. "What?" I asked defensively.

"Oh nothing. It's fascinating to watch you think though."

"Whatever."

Chapter 12

I was furious at being put in the position that I was in. I hated losing my free will even if I might have agreed to the situation. I felt like my hand was being forced. However, I was not so angry as not to see practicality. I figured if I had to stay here, I would enjoy it.

Twenty minutes later I was up to my neck in bubble bath and sighing with bliss. Note to self, the next time I upgrade, ensure that my place as a huge bathtub. I wonder who Jared contracted to build it. It was amazing yet it reminded me of something you might find in a sultan's harem. The most amazing thing was how quickly it filled up. I kept waiting for the water from the faucet to cool down but realized that he must pay a small fortune to have a hot water heater that large.

I couldn't help but sigh happily when I was submerged up to my neck in warm water. Bliss and I closed my eyes. "You look like the cat that ate the canary."

I gasped, "What are you doing here?!?" I sputtered. Jared grinned.

"Visiting my bathroom?" His shirt was carelessly unbuttoned so I could see an expanse of his chest. My heart began to beat rapidly. Jared didn't need the ability to mesmerize to get willing donors. All he had to do was walk around and flash his chest.

"Your bathroom? You're a vampire. You don't need a bathroom." There a good logical argument since whatever made vampires what they were kept them from getting sick or for playing host to a whole host of bad things that make you spell.

"Well technically all the bathrooms in the place are mine but this is my set of rooms that you are set up in. Besides, I like a good soak in the tub whether I need it or not"

"What?!?" I shrieked! "Are you intent upon ruining my career? I can't stay in your rooms!"

"For tonight, yes you can. I promise not to seduce you." He winked, "Unless of course you want me to. But this is the safest set of rooms in the house."

"Oh my God. What is everyone going to think!" I wasn't sure exactly what to do in this situation. I really didn't. I was used to having vampires fight me every step of the way. I was used to being threatened to be killed. But Jared, oh no, he has to talk about seducing me.

"Likely nothing in this day in age. It's not like it was 100 years ago. Or even 50 years. However you are guaranteed complete safety from any monster in this town under my authority. If they were foolish enough before to want to mess with Cassandra James. They would be completely insane to mess with you now."

I watched with fascination as he stripped his shirt off. Holy Jesus, Mother of God! I was on the verge of acting like a complete hussy. There should be a law that reads: Jared MacAllistair is not allowed to go around shirtless in front of unsuspecting women. I swallowed hard and willed some backbone in me. "I need you to go. I need to get out of the bath," It sounded awfully weak to me, breathless, and just a touch desperate.

"Don't let me stop you. It isn't like I have never seen a naked woman before."

"That's not the point," I ground out. "You've not seen me and I want to keep it that way! I need privacy. Now!" I added the last with as much imperious command that I could muster.

"That sure of yourself that you could turn me into a lad overcome by his first wench?"

"Stop twisting my words, Jared. You know damn well that is not what I am intending."

"Suit yourself." He walked out as he was unbuckling his belt.

I hastily scrambled out of the tub and dried myself off and got myself covered with a large terracotta robe that was left for me. I took a deep breath and with mixed feelings prayed he was not waiting for me naked and half prayed that he was.

He was flipping through TV channels shirtless but wearing a kilt. I was disappointed and relieved at the same time. I walked confidently over and sat next to him. Repeating over and over in my head that I was a grown woman and not a teenage girl and that I could do this. "Aren't you curious about what is under the kilt?" He asked confidently.

"I think that I can live without that answer."

"I can tell that you are lying, lass. Why are you fighting so hard against this? Why not just see what happens and have some fun in the process?"

I took a deep breath. "Let's say I toss every rule of professionalism out the window and trample propriety without a care for a bit of fun. Then what? I have to have professional interactions with you later on."

"Let's forget for a moment that you are Cassandra James and I am Jared, the vampire king of Charlotte. Whatever happens in this room from this point on is between you and I and not what our titles and duties dictate. Trust me for tonight."

"Not likely. But don't take it personal. I don't trust anyone."

His hand reached out and cupped my face and I had an uncontrollable urge to spill all of my deepest and darkest secrets.

He just had no clue at how deep, how dark, and more to the point how dangerous those secrets were. Sometimes I felt like I was alone on an abandoned island in the middle of an ocean.

"What a shame, lassie." I swallowed past a sudden lump in my throat.

"I'm sleepy and tomorrow is going to be a busy day. I'm going to bed." I lied. The truth was that I was so far from sleep that it wasn't funny. Then it occurred to me that I had better put some sort of clarification. "I trust you will be sleeping elsewhere?"

"If you insist," Jared said grinning wickedly. I frowned with displeasure. "I made other arrangements.

"Lecherous vampire," I muttered angrily and shut the door to the bedroom behind me. Unfortunately there was no lock. I listened at the door for a few minutes to make sure he stayed put not that I was likely to hear since vampires could move very quietly.

Chapter 13

After realizing how ridiculous I was being by listening on the door I turned around. On the bed was a gray nightgown that was comfortable and serviceable. The neckline and back scooped more than I like but other than that it was perfect. I hastily put the nightgown on just in case Jared decided to just walk into the bedroom. It was a little loose but more comfortable than anything.

When I went to the next room and laid down and tossed and turned for what seemed to be forever but according to the wretched clock only amounted to twenty minutes. The bedroom door opened and Jared was standing there silhouetted by the light.

"You're not tired, lassie. I can hear every move you make in here."

"And what happens if I come into the main room."

"You can watch TV or we can play chess or whatever you like.

"And that's it?"

"That's it. Unless you want more and I promise I will behave most ungentlemanly if the occasion demands it. "

I snorted.

"I am still a man under the monster, Cassandra. I'd be lying if I didn't say that I wouldn't try to steal a kiss from you if the opportunity presented it. However, I am a believer in the word no. I know that for some women are chattel but where I came from in my human life, a woman would just as soon slit your throat if you behaved badly."

"Fair enough," I sighed and got up.

Normally, I kept my hair up off my neck and tonight was no exception. I liked having long hair but leaving it hang was completely impractical. So by the time I realized that my back was fairly exposed it was too late because I heard him gasp.

"Shit," I said with feeling.

I knew what he was seeing. He was seeing the start of an intricate design of a crucifix carved into my back. It would almost be pretty in its horridness except that it was marred with whip marks. It began at the middle of my shoulders and extended down to my tail bone.

"Cassandra what whoreson did this to you? Was it Renaldo?"

I laughed bitterly. "No, Chicago would just kill you and if he had done this to me he would be dead. Besides he lacked the imagination for this. My father didn't much care for a daughter who was a freak."

"What kind of man does that to his own child?"

"The kind that is a right winged evangelical preacher who thought he could beat the monster out of me."

"What's his name?"

"Oh no, I'm not telling you that."

"Well your last name is James."

"Yep."

"Why do I have the feeling that James was not the surname you were born with."

"Nope. And save your breath in tracing my origins. Renaldo already did that and it irritated him to no end that he couldn't figure out where I came from. He is used to being able to find information when it suited him except when it came to me."

"That sounds like a challenge."

"If that's how you choose to view it. But I was merely warning you not to waste your resources."

"You ken, lassie, you are awfully cute when you are being stubborn. Annoying but cute."

"I thought we were supposed to be watching a movie or something."

"You're right. I'm not seeing the full view of your back am I? How far does it go?"

"The shape is a crucifix and it ends at the bottom of my tailbone."

"How long where you tortured?'"

I closed my eyes to fight back the memories that plagued me for years. "Honestly, I don't remember. I kind of lost track of time. But long enough. I'm not interested in talking about this if you don't mind." I hope I didn't have nightmares. I tried not to think about it too much or I was guaranteed to be dreaming about it. My days then kind of ran into each other back then.

He didn't try to steal that kiss even though I fell asleep with my head on his shoulder. One of the myths of vampires is that they are cold because they are the walking dead. But when they are awake they are as warm as you or I. When they sleep however, they lose that body temperature. I recalled vaguely him carrying me to the bed and he might have kissed me on the cheek. What I did know was that I was very much in trouble with him. I relaxed around him whether I liked it or not which meant my guard was not nearly as strong as it normally was. He was as dangerous as Renaldo. Just in different ways. I wasn't so sure if I didn't prefer Renaldo. At least I knew where we stood at every moment.

Chapter 14

I woke to the sound of Beverly Hills Cop playing repeatedly. It wasn't until it rang for the fourth time that I realized that it was my phone and I groaned as I picked it up because it was the ring tone for Detective Anderson.

"Hello?"

"Good morning. What took you so long to answer?"

"You're one of those annoying people who wake up cheerful aren't you?"

"Guilty. My mother said I was cheerful even as a baby. Could you be prepared for a press conference at noon?" Detective Anderson asked.

"I could. What's going on?"

"We got the lab reports back and rushed the latest victim through testing."

"And?"

"Physical proof that it was not a vampire. The toxicology reports came back that all the victims were given the same drugs. A common blood thinner to make it flow easily and a tranquilizer that is more commonly used in zoos so that they were asleep during what appears to be a procedure. Oh and I took DNA swabs around the bite areas and surprise-surprise. They forgot to clean up and the DNA came out as human."

"Did Jared give you the surveillance video for number four?"

"Yes and my team is going over it now."

"You know the good reverend isn't going to like it one single bit.."

"What a shame," he said insincerely, "Cassandra, can you stay at the vampire king's one more night?"

"I would really rather not. You had better give me a good reason"

"The person who broke into your place and set fire cut themselves and it appears based on preliminaries that it might be the same person."

I felt like I had been punched in the stomach. I could just picture it which was unfortunate. If I were to go missing and they find evidence that I had been here. Jared gets the blame. It made sense that if I died from something that appeared to be vampire related because nobody would be voicing an opposition and the entire bloody city would be enflamed. If last night had gone as planned, I would have been victim number 8. Whoever was behind this would have been able to kill 2 birds with one stone and the momentum would have been unstoppable. It would be a modern day witch hunt but there would be no question on who the perceived bad guy would be.

"Cassandra, are you there?"

"Yes. Detective… Jared isn't the primary target. He is the bonus. If I were to end up dead, especially as the 8th victim, Jared would be the obvious fall guy wouldn't he?"

There was a long silence.

"Possibly. No not even possible, he probably would be. I know that I would be expected to think it. But the question is why? You're prominent but not an activist and nobody knows that you're getting on well with the community yet."

"It's personal between me and the Reverend. We've known each other a long time and I deal fairly with the preternatural community. In his book that is as good as being an activist. "

Detective Anderson grunted, "Perhaps. I have a feeling there is more to it than that though."

"I'm going to cancel my classes for the afternoon which will make my students who were up all night cramming ecstatic. They had a major assignment due today and they'd have been up all night finishing it. I'll have a driver take me to the police station."

"Be here by noon which according to my watch is in a little over an hour. That's when the press conference will be."

A note was on the other pillow that I opened it.

Cassandra:

Help yourself to anything you want in the kitchen and instructions have been given to give you anything you ask for.

Jared

I frowned because I knew what everyone from the maid to the horrid butler was thinking. I couldn't bring myself to care very much. I flipped my cell phone back on frowning at power bars.

"Anderson."

"Can you pick me up?"

"Sure thing. Half hour?"

"Absolutely."

I tiptoed out of the room and down the hall. When I entered the kitchen a bunch of lunch fixing were laid out. Presumably for the other members of the house. I quickly made a sandwich to take with me.

When I stepped out the front door, Detective Anderson was already waiting for me. He was disgustingly cheery. "So how was last night?"

"It was alright. Not a fate worse than death."

"If you really can't manage it, I'll pull some strings. Sometimes my department doesn't get the funding that it deserves." Detective Anderson looked a little embarrassed as he said it.

"No, if you need me to stay here another night or two I am alright with that. Jared has been the perfect gentleman."

"Thanks Cassandra."

"You owe me though."

"I won't forget that I owe you a massive favor."

"So what do I need to know about the press conference?" I asked between bites as I scarfed my breakfast or whatever you wanted to call it down.

"Right. We will gather at the Court House since it's purdy and has an iconic look to it. We'll go in via the back entrance and step out the front steps for the reporters. We will give our statements of fact. And then we'll take ten questions. One from each reporter. Then we depart."

"That makes sense. Are we going to the station first or straight to the court house?"

"Given the time, we're going to make a straight trip."

I stared out the window practicing in my head the various answers to possible questions that I would be asked. I wish I had more time to put some makeup on but how I looked really wasn't as relevant as my ability to do the job.

Detective Anderson did not force me to chat. Possibly for the same reason as me. He was practicing his speech in his head.

When we began approaching the court house, the streets were crowded and Detective Anderson groaned.

"We're going to have an audience." He hit his sirens that made it easier to get the rest of the way.

We were escorted down to where we needed to be though I had to admit that I was rather impressed with the building. It was very elegant.

At precisely noon Detective Anderson, myself, and a distinguished man with a horseshoe balding pattern and pencil-like mustache, identified as Lt. Carraway, Detective Anderson's boss stepped out to the flashing lights of reporters.

Lt. Carraway was introduced first and he talked about Detective Anderson's years in law enforcement and that he didn't have any doubt about his abilities. He also was confident in my abilities as I had a long history of being an expert with an accuracy that is unrivaled. All really nice things.

When Detective Anderson then began speaking the only sound you could hear was the sound of the cameras clicking. For someone being as socially awkward as he tended to be, he was a very good orator. He did explain that there had been murders but that they had been working hard to apprehend the perpetrator. That the reason he had not notified the public was because he didn't want to cause a mass panic and that if these attacks had been preternatural in nature that he would have done so. He explained that toxicology indicated that these victims had high concentrations of tranquilizers and the like.

I got to explain what I did. Then it was question time. The questions were general run of the mill on the most part. But one stood out. "Why would the good reverend call you incompetent if you aren't."

I felt a bit of a prickle from the heat of the sun reached to brush a trickle of sweat away and as I reached up to wipe it away and answer, I heard a loud pop-pop and my entire arm exploded in pain and Lt. Carraway knocked me down and knocked the breath out of me in the process.

I heard a lot of screaming as I was dragged inside because for some reason nothing worked. That's when I saw the blood.

"We're going to get you to the hospital. Stay with us."

"It's just my arm."

I saw Detective Anderson roll his eyes up. "You are losing a great deal of blood right now."

For some reason I felt the need to answer the question that was posed to me. "The answer to the question. Because he is a bigot who is incapable of understanding new concepts."

"Seriously, you're answering the question while bleeding?" When he spoke it was a faint buzzing noise and I bit my tongue to try to keep from fainting. But despite my best efforts the world was tinged in a creeping black.

"She's fainted," I heard someone say. I remembered struggling and saying, "Did not," the last thing I heard was a chuckle and the world went black. There are some days when you really are better off not getting up out of bed. This was proving to be one of those days.

Chapter 15

The sound of the beep was annoying but I kept trying to follow the sound. The room was dark but with a bright light coming from a hallway. As my eyes adjusted to the dark I could see a dark figure sitting in a chair with a claymore propped next to him. My mouth was dry like it had been stuffed with cotton. I licked my lips but it didn't seem to help. "Hello?" I finally said though my voice came out weakly.

"You're awake?" I recognized the voice immediately as Jared.

"Jared? What are you doing here?"

"Guarding you."

"What time is it?"

"Almost two in the morning."

"What day?"

"Thursday."

"I seem to have missed a few days. Which week?"

"Same week. You've only missed 3 days."

"Damn. What happened and more to the point why are you guarding me?"

"You were shot and seeing as it was an assassination attempt I offered myself for a shift as the police funding seems to be non-existent when it comes to protecting you."

"Ugh. I seem to be fine now."

"The bullet wasn't make of silver. You should mention that you heal incredibly fast. The doctor thought you might be a lycanthrope but the tests came back negative. You may not even have a scar from it."

"May I have a glass of water?"

Jared got up and poured a glass of water and handed it to me. I took a couple of sips of the wonderful liquid.

"So care to talk to me about how you can scar in some areas of your body, but you heal a gunshot wound like it was nothing?"

"Like you said. The bullet wasn't made of silver. The knife was." Jared's eyes narrowed a bit.

"And?"

"Well perhaps it helped that liquid silver was poured into the wounds themselves." Jared sucked his breath in to that revelation and figured I had better not reveal anymore. I wasn't sure why I even revealed that.

Finally he said, "If you are feeling up to it, I am taking you out of the hospital tonight."

"Why so soon?"

"We're hoping to announce that you survived and the person who attacked you will come to the hospital to finish the job."

"Jared, I can't just disappear."

"Shh...It's only for a few days. You have to stay hidden anyway for a few days at least since the whole thing got caught on camera. You've made an effort to keep your healing abilities quiet because not a whisper has ever come out about it. If you walk out tonight you won't ever stop being asked questions."

There are two types of people in the world that I hate. Those who think they know it all even when they don't, and those who know it all and are dead accurate. Jared just fell into the latter category.

"Besides what makes you certain you can keep me safe?"

"I'm taking you to The Endless Night. My household was preparing for the move there anyway. The security in my compound there is the best. It's why we were moving. The house had to many entrances. There is only one in my compound and each person has their individualized code and a few other checks."

"Won't someone see me leave with you?"

"Well it's not impossible but not very likely."

"I'm not following."

"I find most people don't bother looking up. Especially at night."

"What does looking up have to do with it and more to the point does the hospital know about your nefarious plan?"

"Lassie, there isn't any loop holes in this. You have a preternatural investigation department that is underfunded and a house that has not begun to be repaired. If I let you check into a hotel, yes I will put my best guards and even guard you personally if I have to. However, you are a sitting duck there. It would take an army to get through my defenses at the Endless Night."

I hated logic. It could be a real bitch. "Now to answer your questions. I can fly and can fly you with me. And yes, the doctor, Detective Anderson, and even his boss Lt. Carraway know all about this and even approve. The doctor will check you out once more though we were pretty much waiting for you to wake up."

I recalled vaguely a man in a white coat taking care of me. But only a glimpse.

"The doctor is a lycanthrope?"

"Excellent. You weren't that out of it when you opened your eyes. He was absolutely convinced that you were so out of it that you couldn't even tell."

"I always can tell."

"I'm going to call the doctor in."

"What about everyone else?"

"Everyone else is fine though Lt. Caraway broke his wrist tackling you to the ground."

"Maybe that's why I feel like a truck has been ran over me."

"Perhaps, he was a star quarterback at Old Miss. I'll go get the doctor."

Chapter 16

The doctor was a fussy man with thinning hair that was artfully combed over to hide the patches that had given up the battle to grow hair. I very badly wanted to ask if when he changed he had balding spots or if it was just his human form but I behaved myself. He removed my IV carefully, gave me a pain pill prescription if I needed it and told me that I had to eat when I got to my destination. Jared politely averted his eyes as I slowly changed clothes. I was then wrapped up in a black blanket. Jared strapped his Claymore to his back and picked me up. The doctor opened the window and said, "I officially discharge you. I'll check on you in the morning. You were very lucky."

It occurred to me that my back might have been in full view because I was wearing a hospital gown and I looked at Jared.

"How many people saw my back?"

"And what makes you think there were any?"

"Hospital gowns are known to not close in the back."

"Me, the doctor, and Detective Anderson. Possibly a few nurses. I was invited to look because they wanted a second opinion on what I thought might have caused the scars. Nobody has ever seen the like of it . Also with the way you were healing they wanted me for questions because they weren't sure what you were."

"I'm human."

"Really," he said with deep sarcasm and I flushed with anger.

"Why Anderson," I said changing the subject.

Detective Anderson because he happened to be around at the time."

Jared took a deep breath and said, "Hold on tight.. and don't look down" He stepped out into nothingness and we began to fall but slowly I felt the air change direction. We went way up and when I looked down the cars on the ground were just pinpricks.

It was cold and the city looked like little flashing ants.

"I think we are high enough," and it was as if a breeze was pushing us along.

"How do you do it?"

"I just do. I was only a decade into my life as a vampire when I first flew so it is so instinctual that I'm not sure how to explain it. I probably could do it from the first day as a vampire but didn't need it until I was in a bit of a pinch."

I was cold and the air was slightly damp. I couldn't help but shiver. "We'll be there soon."

I saw the massive structure that was the Mall of the Endless Nights for the first time. It was a mix of a modern day architectural wonder and something out of the middle ages with realistic looking dragons and gargoyles.

"Impressive."

"You think? Let's just hope it is successful."

"Well I understand that there is already an impressive community waiting to move into their newly bought condo's."

It was impressive. There were small oasis throughout breaks in the roof. Towering columns with fierce dragons and gargoyles climbing them. Some so realistic that you almost expect to see the dragons breath fire. When I mentioned it he laughed. "Actually, they are set up so that on special occasions they will in fact breathe fire."

"Brace yourself. I'm about to land."

We landed in one of the gardens near a gazebo. Or what appeared to be a gazebo. It turned out to be a platform that with a touch of a button took us underground. There was nothing special or unique about the hallway. When we reached the door a palm scanner popped up and he placed his hand on it. I heard a click. An electronic voice said: Name. He said his name.

The door swung open to another door. Which opened. There was a guard that was able to see out to ensure that the system had not been duped. Inside the hall was marble and rich furnishings. "Welcome to my compound Cassandra. Are you hungry?"

My stomach growled and I said "Yes. I feel a bit woozy still too."

"Dominica is acquainting herself with her new kitchen. Today is the first time she has had a chance to see it."

We walked down a series of corridors. "Is it my imagination or is this place larger?"

"It is larger. My compound will house close to 200 if I need it too. Right now only 100 will be living here. 25 vampires and 75 were-animals. Many will live in housing elsewhere on The Endless Nights because they want their own space. Guests will stay elsewhere.

"Ah here is the kitchen."

He opened the door and I gasped. It was enormous. There was a door to a huge walk-in and several fridges lining the walls. It was the most elaborate professional kitchen I had ever seen. Dominica was busily stirring something when she looked up and realized

Jared was there. She dropped her spoon that was hastily picked up by someone else to resume the stirring and she ran into his arms. "Thank you! Thank you, thank you, thank you!" She cried happily.

"You have more than earned it."

 "Yes, " Dominica said, "And tonight as my grandmamma used to say in her thick Italian accent "Et ez a especial occasion so tonight I cook French." Of course she would then serve up an Italian dish. If someone dared to question she would look at them and ask, "Are you French?" and if they said no, she would say, "Then what do you know?""

I laughed. "So are we having French tonight?"

"No. Greek!"

Chapter 17

While I was starving I found that I couldn't eat as much as I wanted which was a real shame.

"Let me take you to my chambers. They aren't complete with my furniture but it's close."

"Why can't I have my own? It's not appropriate for me to stay in yours." I asked suspiciously.

"You are perfectly correct, lassie." He said a smoothly. A little too smoothly. "However, the reason for mine is that it's the only one that does have furniture. The compound won't be fully occupied until next week. I promise to be a gentleman."

I wasn't sure if I would ever find my way around the maze of halls. When we arrived to a room with a large door, he opened it and I stepped in. There were some similarities to the other but the colors were different. The layout was bigger. "I have a computer set up. I'm sure you need to correspond with your students tomorrow."

"Yes, I do."

"I'm going to stay just in case you get dizzy. The doctor warned me that you might and it isn't unusual since shape shifters tend to have periods of dizziness if they suffer a significant amount of damage."

I wandered around the suite. It was bigger and rather than just one bedroom to sleep there was a second one both equipped with beds which relieved me. "I won't be staying at the Endless Night tonight." I cursed silently because I couldn't imagine that I was that readable.

The bathroom was huge. It felt like a Turkish harem. When I mentioned he smiled and said that the Moors had the right idea when it came to bathing.

"What did the doctor say about my back?"

"He wondered how given that you will only escape being shot with a faint scar if that, what you had to go through to get the scars on your back."

"I don't want to talk about it. It nearly killed me. My great-grandmother rescued me ultimately. She always knew there were others among the world you know. When vampires were brought out it was no surprise to her. She said she knew it was a matter of time with technology getting more and more advanced."

"May I see the scars again?"

I shrugged though puzzled why he wanted to see something like that.

"If you wish though I don't know why."

"Call it curiosity."

I lifted my shirt in the back so that he could see them. I couldn't help but flinch when his fingers began tracing them with his fingers. I always hated them and was very careful never to show my back to anyone and here I stood with my shirt partially up allowing him to deliberately stare at them.

Eventually, his hand fell. He touched my jaw with a single finger and brought my head so that I was staring at his amazing fierce eyes. "If I ever find out who did this to you, I swear, Cassandra, he'll pay and I have a feeling that he doesn't heal as fast as you. It's just a pity that you're sensitive to silver"

"How do know that I react?"

"Because you heal quickly and it's the only way you would scar is by silver. Now tell me that I'm wrong."

"You are only partially wrong." His eye brow ached in skepticism.

"I react to silver but it is not deadly to me like it is for you. It makes me sick yes. But what nearly killed me with these scars was a combination of infection, dehydration, and being malnourished. Now if you don't mind, I'd like to have my bath and I don't want to ever talk about the scars again."

"Suit yourself."

"Yes I will because you just don't understand how much of a freak it has made me. I have nightmares if I dwell on them too much as well."

"I can guess but you are not a freak. You are special and very beautiful."

I blushed as I pulled my hair up and secured it on top of my head with a scrunchi and closed the door firmly behind me. Again I was shocked at how quickly the bath filled up when I turned the taps on. Then I waded slowly into the pool of hot, frothy scented water, closed my eyes and floated. It was bliss.

I felt the water close over my head when I suddenly sputtered and a great wave of sheer exhaustion hit me and I realized I was in trouble because I lacked the strength to get to the edge. I tried to call out but nothing would come out beyond a whisper. Suddenly Jared was there carrying me out of the water. He set me down on a chair and quickly wrapped me in towels and picked me up again and carried me into a warm room.

"I don't understand what happened?" I whispered.

"The doctor warned me not to let you bathe alone and to keep an eye on you. You're exhausted from healing so quickly."

"That explains it I guess," I whispered. "Wish you had warned me. I might have just did a shower. I'm naked." I closed my eyes in embarrassment.

"Again, a woman's body is just a woman's body. Granted yours is exceptionally beautiful but not anything I haven't seen before."

"I'm not beautiful." Jared turned his back as he handed me a flannel nightgown. "Beauty is in the eye of the beholder I suppose, lassie" he said roughly.

I was so tired that I decided not to argue but made a mental note that soon I would have to point out to him that I was a fully grown woman and not a lassie. Lassie sounded like what you would name your dog. In fact, I was pretty sure there used to be a show about a dog named Lassie.

I struggled to stand up but Jared was there picking me up again and carried me out of the bathroom and into the large bedroom with a huge ornate bed where he put me down. I had to admit it was the largest bed I had ever seen before. A dozen or so could sleep in it and not touch. Well maybe not a dozen but a good number.

I yawned and surprised myself by asking, "Will you hold me until I fall asleep?"

I surprised him when his eyes widened slightly. "Yes, I would enjoy that." This was annoying. I liked being around him and yet I shouldn't. In a way I felt like a traitor to everything I believed in. Tomorrow was a new day. I would do better at keeping him at arm's length.

He climbed in the bed next to me and pulled me against him. The last thing I remembered was the scent of him that reminded me of an ancient wood near the sea and him stroking my back and raising my hand to his lips and kissing it. It was a bad idea but at the moment I couldn't have cared less.

Chapter 18

When I woke up I was a bit disoriented with the time. The two things about being underground that I disliked is that without the sky you tend to lose track of time. The other was that your sense of direction gets messed up. If you're like me and have problems with north, east, south, and west, adding up and down just makes it even worse.

It took me a little while to find a clock though I was dizzy if I turned my head at a pace faster than excruciatingly slow. When I found the clock next to the enormous sized bed with the time it said 8:15 though it didn't specify morning or evening.

I fumbled around but managed to get a light on. I examined my arm and noted with satisfaction that there wasn't going to be a scar. But like healing anything for me, I was completely wiped out. Which was annoying because I didn't have time to be slowed down. The Reverend Monroe had decided to target me at long last openly. Which surprised me at the same that it didn't.

A thistle was lying near me with a note.

Cassandra:

Breakfast is in the main room. Try to eat as much as possible. The laptop in the main room is for you. The doctor will be around when he is finished with his rounds at the hospital. To dial out press 9. To have anything brought to you press zero. The room with the door closed, don't open the door.

Jared

It took me awhile to get up. I wandered into the main room turned and screamed. In a corner there was a man was sitting. He had long black hair and appeared to have a Native American background.

"My apologies miss! I was told to strictly stay here until you woke up. For breakfast!" He said nervously looking anxiously towards to the closed bedroom door. "Jared said he left you a note?"

"It's alright. I wasn't expecting to see anyone."

"I am here if you want an omelet or anything else for that matter, but, I am very good at making omelets."

An hour later, one had to admire Jared. For a vampire who had not bit down on a bite of human food in over 2000 years he seemed to be very in tune with feeding those who didn't have a liquid diet. Which was very curious.

After eating I went to the bathroom to find a fresh set of clothes and a few other necessaries waiting for me like a comb. By the time I felt some semblance of normalcy the fussy doctor from the night before was let in. I didn't get his name from earlier before but couldn't help but note that ironically, it was Doctor Hyde. I wanted very badly to ask about Dr. Jekyll but had a feeling that either the joke would be lost on him or he would be most un-amused. He impressed me as being the later so I behaved myself most reluctantly.

"Do you have any lingering tenderness?" He queried as he expertly examined my arm.

"Not really. This is the fastest I've ever healed."

"Rest today. Eat the major meals and perhaps a snack in between. Tomorrow you should resume normal activities. I'd suggest if you don't want the police to be too freaked out to wear a bandage around your arm. Detective Anderson doesn't buy what I told him about being lucky to get a flesh wound. If you are still dizzy tomorrow, have Jared give me a call and I'll be back to visit you."

"Whatever you say doc." I said and I must have sounded bored.

"Hey," he said sharply, "It's your decision to listen. But if you pass out and end up back in my ward again, I will keep you confined for at least a week and feed you the vilest medicine I can come up with in my arsenal of nasty medicine."

I agreed a little more humbly but really, I had a lot of things to do. One of the most important was to check on my place to see how much stuff I had lost. However, after checking my e-mail messages, sending instructions to my students, I was feeling pretty wiped out. I must have lost a bit of blood. Lunch was a small portable buffet of finger type foods but I didn't mind. I had a s small salad with chicken left behind for a snack.

Eventually, I turned the TV on to a documentary that while sounded interesting put me right to sleep.

Chapter 19

When I opened my eyes next the TV was still on and an amused voice said, "Glad to see you are with us, Sleeping Beauty."

"What time is it?"

"Half past 8."

"How long have you been up?"

"Long enough to listen to your adorable snores."

"I do not snore!"

"Fine, you don't snore."

"I snore?"

Jared raised his hands up, "How am I to answer that question, Lassie? I mention it, you emphatically deny it, out of self-preservation, I agree with you, and then you ask me if you snore? If I say yes you will be angry. If I say no, you will not believe me and be angry."

"Stop calling me Lassie!" I snapped aggravated because he had made an accurate observation.

"Why lassie?"

"I'm not a dog!" I grounded out. He started laughing which just made me want to smack him but I didn't dare to do that. When he was able to compose himself he said very seriously.

"You're far more prettier than a dog so rest assured that when I call you Lassie, it is with the upmost reverence of your beauty."

"Why am I here? Why am I not being hidden away in a hotel somewhere?"

"You heard the reason, Cassandra. The department that you are consulting on is seriously underfunded." I had to admit that I was stunned.

"Well that's ridiculous. How badly underfunded?" I couldn't help but think of the few references that Detective Anderson had remarked upon the department being underfunded.

"Bad enough that I know for a fact that if Detective Anderson had not inherited a bunch of money from an obscure relative, he would be hurting financially because he would not be getting paid."

I read through the lines that Jared somehow was that relative and wondered how Detective Anderson would take it.

"That's nuts. Surely you are mistaken that it is that severe. Every police department has funding issues but they can make do."

"I'm not mistaken, Cassandra. In fact, I fear I might be overstating things. The college didn't want to offer you the job because you had no formal education but the region persuaded them to because it was a win for them."

"But why is it so bad?"

"I have no idea. It's a violation of labor laws at the very least. However, the entire state is like this. Fortunately for Anderson, I am the king here and I do not run my group as a democracy. It was not a popular concept in my lifetime."

Of course not, I thought to myself rather sarcastically.

"Still the real question is why? Why not put me up in a hotel remotely? Why must I stay on the premises of the Endless Night?"

"I could put you up in a hotel. A hotel has windows and no real security system. However, it could be done and I could hope that my own security detail could keep you safe. Here, you are guaranteed to be safe though. I picked the option that had the least risks for the time being."

Just then a knock and the door a cart was wheeled in and a table for two hastily erected.

"Perfect timing Lass who objects to being called lassie."

Before I could get back to the conversation at hand something completely unrecognizable was plopped before me and I took a very hesitant bite but it was good. My great-grandmother was not a great cook which instilled in me a natural suspicion on any unrecognizable food.

Jared was sitting opposite of me and alone it was a bit disconcerting. "You know," I said in-between bites of delicious unknown dish, "You sitting here reminds me of Beauty & The Beast."

I caught a sudden twitch of a muscle in his face. My fork clattered to the dish. "I hope that is because it was a ridiculous observation."

"Oh yes," Jared said with a straight face but sarcastically and I frowned because I detected a thread of anger.

"And since I'm the beast, Cassandra beauty, will you marry me? I'd hate to be assigned to a role and not fulfill it."

I couldn't tell if he was joking or being serious and normally I could. He had totally locked himself away which made me want to think he was being serious and I was about to deadly insult the vampire king of Charlotte. Even if it was possible. One of the uncharted territories that has been being fought at the supreme court level has been marriage between humans and the monsters. If you think the gay marriage debate had been bad, it was a mere warm up to the argument when it came to the monsters. The undead being the specific example. It was argued that marriage was to be only between the living and not the living and undead.

I took a deep breath and said, "Of course not." I saw that tick again and felt compelled to add, "I don't know you very well after all." I was on dangerous footing and didn't know how to get back to what it was before. It was stupid, stupid, stupid to question his motives.

"You should eat. You'll insult Dominica if you don't."

I ate in silence at that point. He didn't speak and I didn't encourage him. There was a tension that was not there before.

When dessert was taken and the dishes were set aside and the server was gone I looked up at him. "You weren't joking where you."

"Not really, my apologies. You were perfectly correct in saying no."

"I don't understand why me though?"

"Just forget it Cassandra." He said standing up abruptly.

"Fine," I said angrily as I stood up too but the next thing I knew Jared had me in his arms as I started to fall. Against my will I wrapped my arms around him to hold on.

"What's wrong with me? I shouldn't be so dizzy?"

"You lost a tremendous amount of blood."

"I must have."

"You should be alright by tomorrow."

"I better, I have a million things to do and an investigation that is waiting."

"Do you want to know more about me?" He said abruptly.

I thought about it. No was on the tip of my tongue but that was a lie and he'd know if I was lying to him. And I was curious. "Yes, I would."

And the tension that had been in the room left.

"What would you like to know?"

"Why do you like watching your were-leopards eating?"

"It's a long story but when I was made I was very strong. We didn't measure time quite as accurately as we do now but it was definitely within the first season of my vampire life that I found that I had an animal to call. I kept it a secret for a while from my maker. I don't think even he realized he created an instant master vampire. It took him a year to realize it.

The thirst drove me mad at times. The first were-leopard I encountered, his name was Marius. He was a simple worker. Strong like all were-animals are. He had a wife and was most reluctant to bring me near her. He recognized what I was. His wife turned out to be another were who was terrified of me but tried to be nice because I could be a real jerk by compelling them to do what they didn't want. Marius had been influenced before by a vampire who had his type as an animal to call and the vampire raped his wife.

Anyway his wife went through all the motions and had pulled a loaf of bread from the oven and trying to behave normal, gave Marius some bread to eat and when he ate the bread I could taste it as if it was in my own mouth. More, it helped my thirst. I gain from my were-leopards and recognized their proximity as a partnership because they give me sustenance. My master did not understand. He was abominable to his own animal to call but didn't criticize me too much because he gained if I gained.

Eventually, I was able to amass my own territories and the were-leopards came to me willingly. It's why Charlotte holds so many. The catch is, it only works for my animal to call. Historically, it ensured that if they found me they would never starve again. "

It was fascinating to say the least. "Your turn."

"What?"

"Tell me something about you?"

"That's not fair. I didn't agree to open myself up."

"I will not reveal anything more about myself unless….."

"Unless what?" I asked suspiciously.

"You do me a favor."

"Define favor. Because if it involves getting leverage with the police or interference in an uncomfortable investigation, the answer is absolutely not."

"Oh no. I wouldn't ask that have you. Your integrity, I admire."

"Okay. For each question that I ask, if you give me a satisfactory answer, then I will comply."

"The first question I gave for free. Ask your next one."

"Melina mentioned that you rarely use the females of your animals for sexual fulfillment. Why? The King of Chicago did all the time."

"Melina is correct though for the record none of my leopards have ever been compelled to fulfill my sexual desires. I've had a few act as such for political appearance. The reason why is because my will can override any of theirs if I were to choose to exercise it. I would fear that my own desires are being forced on the person and I might not even know it. It would be as good as rape and I am not a fan of that. Other master vampires may choose to use their gift of an animal to call to enslave their were-animal's but they are weaker for it because their were-animal's serve unhappily. Mine serve happily because I have centuries of treating them humanely and it has served me well. Now there is the small matter of a favor."

"What do you want?"

"I want to kiss you."

Chapter 20

A pin could have dropped in that instance and you would have heard it. I was caught and I cursed my own stupidity. I should have specified something like that. I should have saw something like that coming. I closed my eyes briefly and took a deep breath.

"Are you insane? I can't let you kiss me!" I finally said emphatically.

"Why not?"

"Let's start with the first reason: professional integrity. It would totally screw my impartiality."

"Your impartiality is already compromised. I don't know what you are but you're not entirely human."

"Gee, you have a way of flattering a girl. You ask to kiss her and then you tell her she is a monster."

"What do *you* want Cassandra? If you don't want me to kiss you I won't. But don't say no for reasons that are not yours."

Dammit! Of course I wanted him to kiss me! I was attracted to him. You had to be a dead stick not to be, and even then I wouldn't make any significant wagers of him not being able to wake the dead stick by puckering his lips. He was gorgeous and if anyone knew how to kiss, he would be a pro because he had a few thousand years of practice!

"Did I not give you good answers?" He asked abruptly and I kept my mouth shut.

Well of course he gave me good answers! He was a day walking vampire that could fly, had his own animal to call, and on top of it all, he didn't always have to have blood to exist! He just told me how unstoppable he really was if he ever took a notion to go bad! And the bloody bastard was just standing there waiting for an answer that was a mistake to give and a mistake to not give. I hated that some bastard decided to shoot me. I wouldn't be here, I wouldn't obviously have been tired enough to walk into a trap that hindsight told me that I had, and I most certainly would not be tempted by Jared MacAllistair!

I took a deep breath and finally said. "Fine! One kiss. Keep your hands from roaming and from now on and in the future if we do this question game, kisses or other intimacies are not part of the bargain."

"If you insist. I shall be a slightly sinister gentleman."

Jared gently brushed one a stray hair off my cheek with his fingers and his eyes were stormy. He was beautiful and mesmerizing. My breath caught in my chest with the idea that I was about to be kissed by one of the most handsome men in the world, and while Jared was a vampire, he was a man too. You just couldn't help but be more than a little flattered by it.

"If you dinna enjoy this lass, I'll have to fall on my sword." He whispered in my ear before his warm sensual lips brushed against mine the first time. They were warm, soft, gentle, and very inviting. Each time he brushed his mouth across my mind it was more demanding. Impatient, I threw my arms around his neck and with one hand touched his head to maneuver a deeper kiss. He groaned and pulled me tighter. His hands carefully placed on the small of my back.

It was magical, it was erotic, and it was quite literally the most passionate kiss I had ever experienced. He tasted of a fine wine that was intoxicating with the elusive hints of what I swear was cinnamon. I should have not given into temptation and curiosity. It was a journey and I wanted more of but it had to end. I wanted desperately for him to take an extra liberty that didn't pertain to the kiss that didn't seem to end because I might be able to stop it at that point. Or who was I kidding, it might just push me even deeper into trouble.

Jared MacAllistair was much, much more dangerous than the Chicago king. I couldn't tell if Jared was trembling or if that was me. He gently disengaged though I groaned in protest and he laughed but I didn't care. I laid my head against his chest as I caught my breath. I finally heard him say, "Bloody hell," and I couldn't have agreed more. Bloody hell definitely covered the situation.

Chapter 21

It was six in the morning when I woke up. I felt great and paced back and forth on the carpet. I ate a hearty breakfast because I was famished. I padded back and forth after the dishes were cleared away. I thought about the events that led me here and ultimately Reverend Monroe. Finally, I dialed Detective Anderson's number. "Cassandra?"

"Yes."

"How are you feeling?"

"Much better than before."

"That's wonderful to hear."

"Thanks."

"What can I do for you?"

"I think it is time to visit Reverend Monroe."

Several seconds of silence followed before I heard him clear his throat. "You think that is wise?"

"Yes and no. Yes because he makes mistakes when he is confronted unexpectedly. He is usually very well rehearsed. No because I'm sure he has something to do with all of this."

"If you're sure, I'm game. When would you like to go?"

"Today would be best. Pick me up around noon? Also I will pay for the hotel myself, but, can you secure me a room somewhere? It's not wise that I stay here."

"Are you alright? Did something happen?"

"No. Nothing has happened."

"If you say so," he said with a lot of doubt in his voice.

"I do say so."

I liked the note of concern and I couldn't very well say that everything was wrong because the vampire king of Charlotte had kissed me and I suspected wanted to seduce me and if he didn't, I was in danger of seducing him.

However, as feasible as it sounded I could help but add, "Someone might question my impartiality if I stay here much longer."

"That's possible. Not likely, but I guess anything is possible."

Yep, I added silently. Anything is possible. I could end up picking the lock to the door that was closed with one of my hair pins or seducing the vampire king whom would be more than willing to be seduced, and then we would all be in a pickle because my partiality would always be in question.

Chapter 22

I looked around for any belongings but realized everything belonged to Jared.

"You're leaving at noon?"

Jared was suddenly there and startled me.

"Yes. Detective Anderson and I will speak with Monroe directly and see if he can give us any information about these attacks."

"But you are not going to come back tonight."

"No. I'm not. My impartiality is being severely compromised."

"Coward." He said accusingly and I blushed. "Why don't you admit Cassandra that you are fleeing because you want me."

"Of course I want you!" I hissed, "but I can't have you and lend my expertise to the police."

"The police who will never pay you."

"Well if they don't pay me, then I have more freedom in dictating my own terms but that has yet to be seen."

"I wager, Cassandra, that you will come up with another excuse later on."

"That's completely unfair."

"Leaving with your tail tucked between your legs is unfair."

"I need time."

"You have an entire lifetime of it. Don't waste it. "

"Bastard!"

"Aye. Even in truth since neither of my parents were married to each other. At least in a Christian ceremony which is what seems to have mattered for the last fifteen hundred years. My people found that the man who shot you has ties to the reverend. I hope you live long enough to come up with another excuse when you dinna get paid for your sacrifices."

He stormed out slamming the door behind him.

Chapter 23

When Detective Anderson picked me up the first question was "What's wrong."

"Nothing, "I lied and he grunted.

"Suuuure." He flashed a grin and wink at me. After weeks of working with him I decided that I should tell him so that if I had to leave suddenly he wouldn't be shocked.

"He kissed me." I blurted out suddenly. Detective Anderson whistled a long whistle and with a grin asked, "So did you like it?" I could feel my cheeks turn red from the question and said a quick, "No."

"Really?!? Imagine that. Being a few thousand years old and still be a lousy kisser."

I felt like if I could crawl under a rock and hide, I would have." Detective Anderson looked over at me and said, "Never mind. You liked it. There's hope for us poor schmucks after all. Live long enough and you eventually learn a few things" I couldn't help but laugh. He was so outlandish in his statements but he did have a sense of humor.

"Well finally. She laughs."

I sobered instantly. "He's going to ruin my reputation and bring questions on my neutrality."

"That's bullshit, Cassandra. There's no such thing as being neutral. Even those who claim they are neutral have an opinion but just lack the balls to pick a side."

"Still it wouldn't do. Everyone knows about Jane Borgman. She fell for a vampire and her career was toast."

"Yes but Jane Borgman wasn't you. She didn't have the abilities but was just lucky. You might find that you can dictate more."

"Perhaps. You know you should be discouraging me from this. What's up with that?"

Detective Anderson squirmed a bit and finally said, "You know the girl, Melina?"

"Yeah?"

"Well I'm kind of sort of seeing her."

"Wow. I didn't see that one coming."

"Neither was I," he muttered before clearing his throat, "We kind of connected when you were in the hospital. She was acting as a liaison."

"Don't you wonder about your position though?"

"Not particularly. They can't find anyone who is willing to take this position. I'm the 9th head of this department and I've outlasted all of them and I've only had it for a year and a bit. They'd keep me no matter what just so they don't have to try to replace me. So what do you want to do first?"

"I think I'd like to see the damage to my place."

"Well I think you'll find that is being taken care of already."

"It is?"

"Yeah, didn't Jared tell you?"

"No. What exactly was he supposed to tell me?"
"He bought the property outright from your landlord and is making the repairs and upgrades."

"Upgrades?"

"The kitchen is being replaced since you lost everything in it. The place was pretty bad. The owner was happy to sell it so that he didn't have to deal with the insurance or anything."

I was furious. Detective Anderson looked at me askance. "Don't be too mad. The place is getting a security system that will make you virtually untouchable. It's really sophisticated."

"Just wonderful. You should see how wrong this is."

"This is between you and Jared. I'm going to stay out of it. So we're going to see the good Reverend Monroe?"

"Yeah I guess so since the rest of my life is being ordained for me."

Chapter 24

When we got to the house that Reverend Monroe was staying at we greeted by a butler whose eyes widened a bit before letting us in. Detective Anderson had to flash his badge but all in all being let through the front door was not that difficult.

We were lead outside to a patio where Reverend Monroe was sitting with his lunch. His eyes widened a bit when he saw me. But otherwise he didn't give a flicker of recognition.

"Detective Anderson," he nodded. "Would you like some lunch?"

"No thank you."

"Then what might I do to assist you?"

"What are you doing here?" I asked bluntly. I heard Detective Anderson take in a deep breath because of how I attacked the problem.

"Why furthering my mission to stamp out evil as you well know."

"Bullshit. You didn't extend your mission to Chicago and we all know that Renaldo is head deep in organized crime there."

"I merely go where God tells me and he told me Charlotte."

"Ah. You really should get seen about that. I've heard hearing voices isn't always a good sign." I was making Detective Anderson more and more nervous. I could hear him shifting back and forth.

I see that you are remarkable recovered from being shot."

"Yeah well, I got lucky. The bullet just grazed me."

"Hmmm." He looked skeptical of it. Of course he was skeptical of it. He knew damn well that bullet pierced me. He also knew damned well why I was healed now.

"What do you know of Elliot Jensen?" Detective Anderson asked.

"Who?" The reverend and I asked in unison.

"Elliot Jensen. The guy who works in your organization and shot Cassandra."

"I must commend him though I have such a large organization. Surely I can't be expected to know each one of my employee's personally though. Or be responsible for their actions?"

Angry I finally said, "Bullshit Daddy!" I said and advanced to him. He had aged over the years. There were more lines than I remembered that perhaps a camera would not pick up.

"Ms. James I have no idea what you are talking about. I reached out and yanked a hair out."

"Detective Anderson, run a test on these hairs and you'll find that I am this man's daughter."

"Outrageous!" The reverend yelled! "You come here and assault me?"

"I'd be very careful, Daddy before you call the guards or your little empire will come crumbling down as you well know because I'm supposed to be dead, remember? It wouldn't do if the entire world finds out that Alyssa Monroe did not die from a vampire attack. That she ran away after being tortured and that her great-grandmother raised her to protect her from you."

My father's face was a deep shade of purple and for a moment I wondered if I had managed to kill him. I know seeing me parade in front of him was quite the shock. "So how's your so called vampire scar? You might not let the media get such good shots of it these days. They might link us together. You wouldn't want the world to find out that the scar of the vampire bite that you sustained trying to save me from the evil vampire that supposedly killed me will fit my dental pattern from back then. Grandma took me to the dentist for x-rays."

I glanced over at Detective Anderson who was obviously dealing with a great deal of shock from my revelations and I would have to apologize for surprising him.

"So you are here to blackmail me?"

"No, actually, I won't make these statements public. Unless of course you force me to. And I am sure you won't do that, will you?"

"What do you want?"

"First of all how is Mom?"

"Well enough," he said shortly.

"That's good. So let's chat about why all of a sudden you are trying to kill me? I haven't ever gone public about our little relationship or at least not yet, per your agreement with Granny. I don't look like you and our names have never been linked.. at least not until now. If a reporter goes digging and it all comes out, it will be your own fucking fault."

"None of this was my idea and the individual who came up with the idea has no clue at who you are to me," He said shortly.

"But you didn't fight it."

"No, I admit, I am guilty of that sin. If you were in fact dead I wouldn't have to worry about any truths coming out. However, while I do not view you as my child, I would not personally put an order out for you."

"I really hate being shot at. But that explains why they didn't use a silver bullet. If you were intent you would have made sure the person knew to use silver."

Detective Anderson was looking more and more confused. I so owed him an apology for springing all of this on him.

 "So is it coincidence that these murders are happening because I came to town?"

"One could make a direct link," He said carefully and I saw a flick of fear in his eyes. He got up and said, "come to the side with me."

I followed. Detective Anderson wanted to go but I stopped him with a finger."

"Maybe I can tell you. I can't talk about it. But listen to me," he pulled me close so that he could whisper in my ear, "we've sold our souls to the Devil and didn't realize it. A vampire is behind these attacks. He gave us the idea and the detailed plans."

"Which vampire?" I prayed he wouldn't say Jared.

"I don't know. But he hates his own kind. He liked it when they were out of the public spotlight."

"Jared?"

"Of course not girl! Don't be stupid," he snapped. "Didn't I say I had no idea who it was? Talking to you will likely be the death of me."

"He wants me dead?" I whispered.

"I believe so. He seems to be afraid of you for some reason."

"Have you met him?"

"Yes. But I can't recall his face."

"He managed to mind fuck you?"

"He's old. Very old. So old that my bones ached." Realization dawned on me that he had to be gifted to feel that.

"You bastard. You called me a monster but you have some of my gifts."

"Some but untrained. I turned my back because I do believe they are an abomination. I realize that yours were such that you could not ignore them. I didn't understand at the time but Grandma certainly spelled it out. Can you kill something this old?"

"I'm not sure."

"How powerful is this Jared of yours?"

"Fairly."

"Enough to save your life?"

"Why?"

"Forgive me child but it must appear that I am not giving you information." Without warning he grabbed one of my silver knives and plunged it in me. I grunted and began to fall. I saw a dark shape fly past me and recognized it as Jared.

"Don't kill him," I whispered. Jared let out a stream of curses but stopped.

"Cassandra, I think he nicked your heart, this smells like a death wound and you're losing a lot of blood fast," Jared said urgently. "I must give you some of my own blood or you will die."

"No," I whispered weakly but knew he was right. The blade nicked me if not my heart something important.

"I swear that I would not tie you to me such if there was another choice."

"I won't become vampire?"

"Nay. But you will be closer to becoming my human companion. But hurry. Or else I won't have any choice but to force you to become one. Companion or vampire."

I drank. It was a coppery taste that kind of gagged me but I drank as if my life depended on it. "That's enough. He pulled his hand back."

I felt a little better. "Don't kill him."

"You little fool, " he whispered.

"There is a master vampire in town that is the mastermind."

Jared looked confused. Detective Anderson was by my side looking concerned and I heard sirens in the distance. I was going to pass out and suddenly all was dark.

Chapter 25

I ached and kept going in and out. The first time I swam out of the darkness was sounds of sirens and orders for someone to stand back. Detective Anderson's voice shouted, "No! He is not the problem." Time was being measured in heart beats. My heart kept faltering but it would seem to be jolted awake.

The next time I came to I heard arguing. "What do you mean you can't continue?" I recognized Detective Anderson's voice who was angry. Angrier than I ever heard. It was hard to believe he could sound so angry.

"Even I have limits, Anderson. Even I can run out." Jared said wearily.

"What if you make her one of you?"

"I'd rather not."

"Why not? You've had no issues of making vampires in the past have you?"

"Aye. I have. But I would rather have absolutely no choice and her consent."

"Well that's a little hard when she is dying." Detective Anderson said sarcastically.

I wanted to scream that I would rather die than be made a vampire. I struggled to open my eyes and saw Jared standing facing a window.

"Again, mi' lord?" A voice that I should place asked. There was a very long pause before he said, "Yes. Leave us, Anderson. For now I am still trying to save her."

I heard a door slam. My eyes were so heavy they closed on their own and I felt a finger touch my cheek.

"I ken what you want Lassie." I would have sighed with relief if I could but the darkness claimed me again. Somehow Jared knew what I wanted though. I had to trust him not to go overboard.

I woke again a million heart beats later or was it just a minute? I didn't know but it was another argument. I wish I could have been able to tell them to shut up.

"Damn you! Why won't you change her?!?"

"Because! She doesn't want it!" The voices seemed to be screaming.

"How do you know what she wants and doesn't want?"

"I just do, Anderson."

"But she can't die" Anderson said frustrated.

"I assure you, she can, and without me she should have. One last time and that is all that I can give."

"MI 'lord, I don't know if that is a good idea." The other voice said.

"Then it's a good thing that it's not up to you," Jared said shortly. The darkness claimed me yet again.

I was either dead or dreaming because I was standing in a field barefoot. I could feel the grass and dirt between my toes and in the distance was my great grandmother. We were out in the woods near the old house and she had her big walking stick. Everyone in the small town near us called her a witch and they were right. She was the wisest person I had never known. She was a tiny woman with long white hair that she kept pinned up nearly all of the time.

But she was always spry on her feet and just as she did in life she was walking towards me with purpose.

"It's a fine kettle of fish you've landed yourself into Cassandra dearie."

"Whatever do you mean?"

"Consorting with were-animals and vampires! Well it was bound to happen I suppose. Our abilities have always put us in the path of the preternatural. Even when they weren't supposed to have existed."

She stumped around a bit. "Do you remember what I told you about the ones that are so old they make your bones ache?"

"Don't try to fight them," I whispered.

"Yes dearie but remember this. If you were to win such a fight don't accept that dead is dead. Sever the head from the body and immediately drag the head away. Don't let it even look at the body that it was for. Keep it in darkness. Take the heart and burn it. Burn the head in a different fire. The ashes will go into different bodies of water. If you have to drive a thousand miles make sure those bodies of water do not connect. Maybe I am just being a paranoid old woman, dearie, but the one that make your bones ache, take nothing to chance. You're different than me. Stronger. You might win such a fight. There is more to you."

"How on earth does one win a fight such as that?"

"Tap into your abilities. Open yourself up and borrow any and all energy in the area if you need to. Even the one who aches if necessary."

I remembered what happened at Jared's when I fought with him with a sword. "Am I dead?"

"Course not. If you were you wouldn't need to ask that question."
A million questions sprung to my mind and then I finally asked
one that had been on my heart for a long time.

"Did you ever love me?"

"What a thing to be asking. I took you in didn't I? Finished raising
you up I did. Taught you all that I knew. I was content to let the
last bit of knowledge die with me as it always seemed to get us in
trouble more often than help us. However, times are different. We
no longer know secrets that everyone else does not. The vampires
and monsters are coming out in the open and that which was myth
is now reality. You're the only one of my descendants to have the
full range of gifts and not try to ignore them. Of course I loved
you. But you didn't need kisses, hugs, and coddling. You needed
to be taught how to survive and I was terribly old. My time was
approaching and I knew it just as I always knew when the seasons
changed. It was deep inside my bones. Didn't have much time did
I? I barely had enough. "

"What should I do about Jared? It's so complicated."

"Yes you are neck deep in it, ain't you? All things will work out in
their own time. He has the potential of being your greatest friend,
love, and ally or he could be your worst enemy and destroy you.
You will have to decide which he is for I will not tell you. You
must guide your own destiny and stop worrying about others. That
might end up being your greatest lesson to learn is to stop worrying
about what is proper and what is not . It is time for you to wake up.
Don't be a slugabed, gel."

"Granny?" I called but swirly mist rolled in and all of a sudden I
was alone.

Chapter 26

I floated in darkness for a while but a noise kept bugging me. The more I concentrated on the annoying noise the louder it seemed to get until I opened my eyes. I wasn't sure where I was so I kept concentrating on everything. As my eyes adjusted, I realized that the sound of the beeping was a monitor and that I was in a hospital room and it all came flooding back in.

"Your awake lassie?" It took me a minute when I realized the deep voice that asked me belonged to Jared asked.

"Yeah. I am."

"Mind explaining away why I didn't kill the bastard?"

I laid awake for a minute. "Give a minute to finish waking up."

"I have all night." After a minute I finally asked, "He's alright then?"

"Unfortunately. Give me leave and I can rectify the situation."

"No. Don't kill him."

"Why? He deserves it."

"He does but he gave me information."

"Yeah. Pity you passed out before you could share the details."

"A master vampire is here in town. One that you might not be aware of. He's behind the murders."

"I don't buy it. I would know for one and if he did those murders, you would know wouldn't you?"

"Of course I would know but he didn't commit them. He never touched the victims. He planned them and rather than indulging himself, he had humans do the job."

"Detective Anderson seems to think that he is your father."

"Who?"

"You know who. The Reverend."

"I owe Detective Anderson an apology for springing that on him. My father doesn't react well to surprise. On the other hand, look on the bright side. My father was having a very bad day. "

"You did say that your father didn't much like unique abilities and was a bigot. You might have mentioned that he also lead one of the top anti-monster hate groups in the country. How can you not let me kill him for hurting you?"

"Because it's not the right thing to do."

"So there is supposed to be a vampire who is after you and that I can't tell that is in my territory."

"That's it in a nutshell."

"It sounds like a load of bollocks to me."

"What if he was older than you and that concealment is his gift?"

Jared frowned at that. "Perhaps," he said shortly.

"Old enough to make human bones ache?"

"I don't know any vampire that can do that. It's possible I suppose ultra-old but none that I've ever met."

"That you know of is a valid point."

"Point taken. If there was a vampire that old, there is a chance that they could hide themselves from me. But it's a very small club and one that is European based. I'm the oldest in North America."

"That you know of." I couldn't help but pointing out. Jared frowned and shot me a dirty look.

"That I know of," he conceded with a grimace, "but you really want me to know of it because a vampire that strong could challenge me for my territory and would make Renaldo look like a cake walk."

The darkness was taking over again and I was exhausted. I buried my head into my pillow and murmured, "I miss my sheets."

"Aye lass," Jared said brushing my cheek with his finger.

Chapter 27

When I woke again, daylight was streaming into my room. Detective Anderson was sitting in a chair.

"What time is it?"

"It's three in the afternoon."

"Of which day."

"You gave us all quite the scare, including Jared I believe and I didn't think that was possible."

"What day?" I repeated more firmly.

"Thursday."

"That's only a day."

"Hey, you asked what the day was. You didn't specify the week."

I resisted the urge to grind my teeth.

"Fine, what week?"

"You've been in the hospital for a week."

"A week!?!" I sat up a bit dizzy.

"A week and it should be much longer. It's going to be much longer publically." Detective Anderson said firmly. "We nearly lost you. It was literally Jared's intervention that saved you, you know."

"I remember he gave me some of his own blood. You were arguing with him"

"You heard that?"

"Yep. For the record I would have made you my first victim if he had just because I would be pissed off with you."

"Understood. But you were near death. Close enough that there was a danger in changing you by accident."

"Out of three infusions?"

"Two? Oh no, not two infusions. He gave you six, Cassandra."

I was speechless for a moment. "Six?" I couldn't even begin to fathom it. No vampire had ever donated that much to anyone to my knowledge.

" It's been good working with you." I finally said.

"What do you mean?"

"I'm compromised, most likely for life."

Detective Anderson just laughed. "So you're going to quit over something silly like that?"

"Silly? I hardly think it is silly."

"Of course not. Oh I'm sure there will be those that will think you should. However, those would rather have something to complain about publically then to do the job themselves."

"Fine. I won't resign but remember that I volunteered it and that you're the one who talked me out of it."

"So noted," he said with a grin.

I noticed that I didn't have an IV or anything hooked up in me.

"When can I leave?"

"When you're ready. It's been a matter of when you wake up. Though you have visitors who want to see you."

"Who?"

"The DA has been very anxious to see you."

"The District Attorney?"

"Yes. Your father has been charged with attempted murder."

"Also there's a representative from your students waiting with most of your students. The college students came in shifts while you were out. They've even been so kind as to use your injuries to write a report in your absence. The school was set to cancel the program for the semester but the students insisted they could progress and demonstrated quite convincingly that they could self-guide themselves. They even interviewed Jared who made himself available. I hate to say this Cassandra but I believe that your students are going to end up being the best and the brightest in the country."

"But I've only met them a few times."

"You left quite the impression. You're going to get 15 reports and presentations on your injuries."

"Be honest with me. How close was it?"

"Well this is what I can tell. He thrust the blade in to appear that he was going for the heart but he was off by just a bit. He did nick the heart though which is why you kept losing blood. You weren't healing fast either. But the reverend was not making a real attempt to kill you. He was horrified when Jared wasn't able to heal you on the spot.

You nearly died. You should be dead. Jared put a lot of personal risk to save you. He gave you so much that he would be endangered himself of a real death. If you had not taken it, I can professionally say that you would not have made it. Jared said that you might have more amplified gifts now but we won't know until later. "

"Well I don't feel any different right now." I remarked almost to myself.

"You're not near Jared yet. Even unconscious, your body responded differently when he was in the room after that much. That resignation offer might be a reality but until I know what happens, you're on the job. However, I don't envy you. I suspect both you and Jared are fucked."

I sighed because how could you argue with the reality? I was starting to think that maybe I had been better off in Chicago after all.

Chapter 28

The first of my visitors arrived in the form of my students. They huddled around me and peppered me with questions. They had me show them the wound that had nearly healed and even the arm that had been shot earlier. Exasperated I finally asked why the questions. At that point Jane, the youngest with short curly hair and spectacles responded. "It's a learning experience. You're the first person we've encountered that has the effects of vampire blood in their system. It's been a wonderful learning experience. Why it even healed where you had been shot. You don't even have a scar."

I realized that the gunshot wounds rapid healing from the outside was perceived to have been Jared's doing. How extraordinarily convenient. Detective Anderson whom appointed himself to stand guard looked like he was going to die from suppressed laughter and I couldn't help but feel resigned that I was in their eyes a human guinea pig.

My second set of visitors came in the form of a short bald man with a polished head that gleamed and his wiry companion. He was so short that I wondered if I might not be at least the same height and with being barely five feet one, I was not breaking any records. His head was so shiny I could almost swear that I could use his forehead to apply my makeup and I suppressed the urge to ask because I figured he would likely be mortally insulted. He had a deep baritone voice that certainly didn't match his height and it was a very authoritarian voice. "It's good to see that you are finally awake, Ms. James. I'm Edgar Hastings the district attorney."

"Hi. Please call me Cassandra. When I hear Ms. James I look for my great-grandmother."

"We're going to bury the bastard."

"Which bastard?" I asked with innocence because Detective Anderson had warned me what the conversation was going to be all about.

"The Reverend Monroe." He said with a very suspicious look at me.

"His parents weren't married? Well wonders never cease. A hypocrite even in that."

Detective Anderson went into a coughing fit, the wiry assistant dropped something that he had to pick up in order to hide his grin, and Edgar Hastings just stood there frowning.

"Young lady, if I didn't know better you were trying to change the subject, but since you are well known to believe in truth and justice I wouldn't expect that would I?" He gave me a pointed look. "What I am here for is to assure you that the Reverend is going to go away for a very long time." He oozed confidence that somewhat annoyed me and while it was petty, I rather enjoyed bursting his bubble.

"No you're not." I said cheerfully.

He frowned and said sternly, "But it's in the bag. There were witnesses that saw him clearly stab you."

"Were they all psychic?"

"N-no." It was then that he realized that he might be over his head after all.

"Well I am and he was being controlled by a foreign master vampire that has entered the area and we need to track down. "

"You won't testify against him?" He asked

"Of course I will testify. It would be my civic duty," He smiled for a second, "For the defense." He frowned at that.

"But he nearly killed you! He hates you and has been trying to make you look like a bumbling idiot before the media and I have to say he is doing quite a good job at it!"

"Is it a crime to really dislike someone and attempt to discredit them?"

"Nothing criminal."

"I have no love for the man. However, I know what right is and what is wrong. He had no choice in what he did. I'm feeling all of a sudden tired."

I turned over. Detective Anderson whispered, "liar, liar, pants on fire". The DA was most perturbed. I had taken his favorite case away and the door slammed behind him as he exited the hospital room.

"No, I am a little tired." I said truthfully. I felt a small surge that was gentle and my eyes flew wide open. What the hell was what.

The door opened after a short quick knock that wasn't really asking permission to come in so much as it was an alert that someone was going to come in.

"Jared is awake. I just felt him wake up." The doctor that entered was the same fussy thin haired doctor that took care of me the last time.

"I felt a little tingly jolt down my spine. Will I know when he wakes based on that?"

"How remarkable," the doctor said. "Well he did give you quite a bit of his blood so it would make sense. He will be taking you to your home which is completely safe and finished. I will visit you to check up on you. Take it easy." I didn't question my house being finished and ready for me to go back. If they can build houses from the ground up in under a week, he could fix my home in that period of time.

 "I'm hungry."

"I imagine there will be something to eat at your place already prepared and really, do you want to eat the hospital food?"

He had a point. "Besides you have one more visitor."

"Who?"

"You'll see. She's been trying to get in ever since you arrived."

She?

Chapter 29

Detective Anderson left the room and she walked in. I had imagined over the years what it might be like to meet but figured it was a box that had best be kept shut. She was the same as I had remembered but older. She had always been just slightly taller than average. Her hair used to be a pale blonde but there were streaks of silver now that were swept up into the bun that she customarily kept her hair in. I couldn't remember more than once or twice with her hair down as hard as I tried to. But underlying there was a thread of anger. Anger that she blinded herself and sat meekly by like a good little wife would do. "What are you doing here?" I demanded a little more harshly than I had intended.

"You nearly died." She said simply. "At his hand."

"Yes. That does seem to be a trend."

"But you refused to allow the attempted murder charge. Why?"

"I could have, but it would have been wrong in this case."

"He would have deserved it. I don't understand since while I don't know everything I can piece some of it together. None of it looks pretty either.

"Honestly, I don't know. I should hate him enough. He would have had no defense. As Hastings made clear, it was an open and shut case. The only persons who knew intent was myself and him. I should want to see him utterly ruined and destroyed. If for no other reason to shut him up. He spreads poison and bigotry unnecessarily. I just want him and his organization to leave me the hell alone and while I'm at it stay out of my way."

"I was told that you were killed by vampires, you know."

"Yeah I know. He does like to brandish the bite mark from his unfortunate encounter. The story is very well known."

"Your funeral was close casket presumably because it was a horrible site to see. I was not allowed to see the body. I was told that it was too gruesome. That it was better than I remembered you as you were."

"I know what you were told. It was in an interview. "

"Why did you never try to get in touch with me?"

I got up and pulled my gown up over my head and turned my back.

"This is why. I barely survived this. I thought it was best just to leave it be."

She gasped and was truly horrified by it which went a long way in helping me with my own feelings. "What has he done?" she said in a voice that was completely stunned. She had no idea what exactly had happened. She swallowed and added, "His grandmother was a strange one. We rarely ever saw her so for her to appear at the funeral was unusual."

"She was good to me. Not very affectionate but good. She taught me how to use my abilities to my advantage. She didn't have many years to train me."

"I am as guilty as he. I should have known," She said simply frowning slightly. "I knew you were alive for the last three years but didn't seek you out. I always figured you had your reasons. I'm leaving him you know."

"You will be a fool. It would lead to questions on why. Especially since it was me that he tried to kill. Some enterprising reporter will put two and two together. It'll be difficult but not impossible. I'd rather our true relationship remain hidden. I have a feeling my entire safety will depend on it."

"He wouldn't dare harm you again!" She said fiercely which I had to admit surprised the hell out of me.

"No. He would try to destroy my career. But how many members belong to his organization? Are they all sane or could it be that more than one are fanatics? That' the problem with lies and poison. You can't control who hears them and what they will do with it. No. I'd rather nobody learn of my true identity thank you very much."

"But I want to be part of your life!"

"Oh mother!" I said exasperated. "It's a little too late for that now don't you think?"

I saw her flinch but sometimes the truth is ugly. "You thought the same as he. That I was a freak. I heard you talk about your child that was very fey like and wondered where on earth it came from."

"Yes! But I didn't want to see you harmed and I certainly did not want this! I see you and wonder if perhaps I might have somehow been mistaken. That perhaps rather condemning that we should have made some sort of effort to understand first."

I laughed. "You know what the real irony of all of this is?"

I saw her blank look of confusion. "He had me tortured me and I would have killed me if I had not managed to escape his little room. He did all of this because I was something other. But he has much of the same gifts that I have." I was laughing so hard tears were streaming down my face and my chest hurt. Detective Anderson looked over at me with a great deal of concern.

"I'm sorry if this puts you in danger but I will not go back to him. I will say that while there might be some truth to your story that God would not have allowed him to do what he did if he had been true. But he has cost me far more than I ever wanted to pay and he has done it twice. At least I understand now why he always changed the channels when you came on or they talked about you. You look like neither one of us."

"Then how did you figure it out?"

"He had a miniature of his grandmother. You could have posed for it."

I leaned forward as to embrace her. "Do whatever you need to do for you Mother but remember this, he had no choice in stabbing me. He passed on information on a major crime spree here and if he had been caught passing information to me, you would all be dead. The knife accidentally nicked my heart. It wasn't meant to nearly kill me. Even the doctor says so. That is why I am willing to lie for him even if his actions have complicated my life in the worst ways now."

She nodded and wordlessly walked away with her held high and I had to respect that. Perhaps she didn't know what was going on. Or that she is trying to get absolution for her past sins from me. I was not in the mood for absolution. The fact remains that she turned a blind eye. All that lingered in the room was the scent of her perfume.

Chapter 30

It was several hours later and twilight had fallen away to dark. I was wearing pants which was something I absolutely loathed to wear. I found pants to some extent restrictive. I could hide much more weapons behind a skirt than I could pants and nobody would realize the extent of what I was carrying. However, I had to admit that I was impressed. They were leather and fit me perfectly. I didn't know how Jared managed to do it but he did. The other thing that I was impressed was that even though the pants were leather, they didn't feel like they were going to stick to my skin like glue.

When Detective Anderson informed me that Jared would be picking me up I refused adamantly but during my time in the hospital my townhouse was back to normal with a few "improvements" which annoyed me since if there were any improvements I wanted to oversee them. However, the important thing was that I was going to go home.

I was standing at the window looking out waiting to see Jared in the sky until I heard a low whistle.

"Ye should wear trousers more often lassie. It becomes you."

I turned around and saw Jared casually leaning against the frame of the door with his broadsword out. His blue eyes were glittering in the semi-darkness of the room. I couldn't help but notice that he was covered in leather and I had to admit he looked good in leather. Was there anything that the man wore that didn't look good on him?

"I thought you were flying."

"No. I cannot fly right now."

"Are you alright?" I was concerned because if he had lost his ability to fly he could lose other abilities that kept him safe.

"Aye. I gave quite a bit of blood to you and it weakened me. I'll be back to normal in a few weeks. Until then a different mode of travel."

I got a little nervous and asked, "What type."

"Motorcycle."

"No! Absolutely not." I couldn't come up with a reason why not but that shouldn't matter should it? The simple fact was that I didn't like the idea of riding anything that involved two wheels and nothing around you to protect you in the event of an accident. I didn't even like to ride a bicycle when I was younger. And all for the exact same reasons!

Jared looked immensely amused.

"You'll be perfectly safe. Trust me."

"Not likely," I snorted quickly. He laughed with amusement. "The Cassandra James is afraid of a mere bike?"

"Absolutely, so let's find a different method."

"It's the best way to protect you, lassie." He said with a note of exasperation when he realized how serious I was. "A limo can only go so fast and maneuver only so quickly. Even with my sword, I would be hard pressed in a fight to defend you in a limo or I would not subject you to it. But my Bike is comfortable, safe, and fun.

He was talking sense. I could continue to stand and fight about it but I knew that I was going to end up on that damn bike if I wanted to go home.

"Fine. But if I get so much as windburn it is your fault," I grumbled. And I stalked down the hall with him laughing behind me. Detective Anderson was at the elevator suppressing his own mirth. "You know Anderson, your warped sense of humor is going to get you in trouble one day."

"It's bound to one day, Cassandra but today isn't it."

Chapter 31

Now I know next to nothing about motorcycles. However, there are things that I do know. I know that Harley Davidson is one of the best out there and without knowing the technical details Jared's bike was both terrifying and very nice looking.

Terrifying because it was huge and would be equally loud. Nice because the paint on it was an electric blue that reminded you have lightening flashing across the sky.

The one thing that I noticed about motorcycles is that riders tended to be like dogs. Sure they could ride alone but they liked to travel in packs. I kept that observation to myself so as not to be too insulting but I could not help but notice that there were six other equally impressive bikes with leather glad individuals waiting near Jared's.

Jared picked me up and sat me down on the back of the bike. Sometimes I hated how the monsters had supernatural strength. I hated it the most when it was being directed against me, admittedly, but even when it wasn't, it still was annoying.

He handed me a helmet. When I asked why he wasn't wearing one he replied, "Vampires and the like are exempt from any helmet laws. We're indestructible. At least by conventional things like being knocked off a motorcycle. Wrap your arms around me and hold on tight."

"If I didn't know better you chose this method for that." I muttered.

"I'll try not to enjoy the fringe benefits, lassie."

"You do that."

The motorcycle roared to life and it was probably a good thing that Jared was the undead because if he had been human, I would have squeezed the life out of him. I felt like I was going to be vibrated to death and it was cold. Autumn was most definitely upon us and while the temperature was not very cold, it was freezing on the bike despite the sheer size of Jared blocking the vast majority of the wind.

My eyes were squeezed shut and after a while I was brave enough to open them for a bit to see the city lights flash by me blurrily. I averted my eyes and saw that the other bikes when possible flanked us on either side and that the various movements. I started getting sick in my stomach and closed my eyes again hoping that we'd get to my place soon. I was so cold that my bones were aching.

Something kept bothering me at the edge of my mind when it dawned on me.

"JARED!" I screamed. "He's here watching us!"

"What?" He yelled back over the sound of the bikes.

"We're being watched. My bones ache."

I prayed to whatever deity that would listen that Jared would believe me and not question it. I felt a frustrated searching that came from Jared and at the next exit all of us veered off keeping formation as much as possible.

Jared growled, "I can't find the bastard. Any clue where he would be?"

"Above us? Would he be able to fly?"

"Possible. Damnation!"

I could feel his frustration and I ached on until it suddenly disappeared.

"It's gone," I half whispered and Jared heard me.

It seemed like forever before we arrived at the street my townhouse was on. He stopped at the street.

"Check lass to see if it's safe for you to go home. You can apparently detect this bastard and I would rather he not be waiting for us at your front door."

"Nothing."

"Good. When we get there, let me lift you off the bike. I wouldn't want you to burn yourself on the pipes."

"G-good," my teeth were chattering because I was so cold.

We pulled in mass into my driveway area. I was sure the neighbors were going to love it but it was done quickly enough and as soon as they got there, the bikes were turned off. So even if we disturbed the neighbors it was over quickly enough.

The first thing I noticed were the cameras and flood lights that came on as we moved towards the entrance to the house. The second was the security system.

Jared punched a bunch of codes in and then said, "Put your hand on the screen."

I did without question just hoping that I could hurry up and get inside.

"This security system, it matches fingerprints. Even if you have a key, it won't undo the deadbolt until you've actually passed the print test. Also if you are under duress, when placing your hand on the screen, if you gently press down three short pushes followed by

3 long firm ones, followed by three shorts, everyone will know you are in trouble."

"What is the significance of the sequences?" I blurted out.

"Morse code for S-O-S."

The door opened and I walked inside my place. It was like coming home to find the home you knew had completely disappeared and another put in its place.

My kitchen area was now more open concept with all new appliances. Instead of a creamy rug, I had hardwood flooring with various rugs. The decorating matched my style so I couldn't be very angry over it all. Key pieces of my furniture were gone and replaced by new. When I inquired Jared said, "Temporary furniture, the cleaner is still working with your furniture but if they can't repair the pieces you can keep these pieces or select ones of your choice."

I wanted to be angry. It was irrational since logically he was only trying to help. However, somehow it seemed incredibly wrong. It was inappropriate. Yet if he hadn't helped, I would be in a hidden place. Gods forbid even ensconced in the Endless Night.

The second biggest change that I noticed was in the bathroom. No matter how angry I was which was unusual for me, even I had to appreciate the changes there. I had a garden tub now and a separate shower.

"I guess this is restoring it to the original state?" I asked with a bit of sarcasm in my voice.

"Nope. I made the upgrade because I could."

"I want to be angry. No, I am angry. Furious. But it doesn't make any sense."

"Nope it doesn't," he said cheerfully. "But it doesn't have to make sense, Cassandra. The end results is that you get to be at your own place and that I have personally made sure it is as secure as it possibly can be short of you living in my compound at the Endless Nights."

"Any idea of who the vampire is?"

"A few more. He flies. Believe it or not that narrows the field significantly. Unfortunately, while you have the luxury of your own home, it also means you will have 24/7 security until this is over with."

I couldn't help but frown at it but realized that he was right and I didn't have much of a choice. I wasn't sure if I would be able to survive another attempt on my life so soon afterwards.

Chapter 32

I'd been given strict orders to take it easy and for the most part it had not been very difficult because I tired very easily. I hadn't seen or really heard from Jared over the following week which was a relief and upsetting all at the same time and I couldn't even put a finger on why.

However, I did have the promised security though they were very close mouthed about everything to do with Jared and the hunt. Detective Anderson, I suspected was part of my body guard detail because he visited often with some news.

My father had been released from jail much to the reluctance of the DA who was publically unhappy with the turn of events.

Detective Anderson warned me that I had made an enemy in him and not to expect my life to go easy when it comes to the courts on the times I had to testify. Particularly if I were on the wrong side of the aisle.

I ran all of my classes remotely and found the confinement completely annoying. I chaffed at it because I knew and Jared knew that if I were in proximity of this vampire again, I might be able to detect him when Jared couldn't. Unless of course the vampire was putting out the welcome mat specifically for me. I did have to take that in consideration.

In the meantime I spent my time getting acquainted with my body guards. I had four named Peter, Matthew, Mark, and Luke. And the first thing I learned is not to ask about where John was. But honestly, it was so worth it. All of them were lycanthropes and personal guards of Jared himself though he didn't really need any but the vampire world was a bit showy.

After I learned not to twit them over their New Testament names, they turned out all to be good. Naturally all of them where fairly big guys. Again the vampire world is a bit showy so it wouldn't do for Jared's official body guards be below average in height. The only one that was as tall as Jared was Mark. The rest hovered around six feet one.

They were like most body guards. Grim and non-descript exteriorly. They wore men-in-black type suits, had short cropped military style hair, and probably a bunch of hidden weapons. Your typical body guard. However, they were individuals.

Again, Mark was the tallest but he actually had a masters in criminology. He was also the most senior of the guards.

Matthew was a playboy and was a confirmed flirt. He even flirted with me when he relaxed a bit. And I could definitely see his appeal. He was tall, muscular, and had the greenest eyes I'd ever seen. So green that you didn't notice his black hair that framed them perfectly. Luke had brown eyes, black hair, and a bit of a Native American look about him. He was also well versed in survival tactics and had seen actual combat. However, the day he became a lycanthrope he was expelled from the military. Peter was the oldest at 42 and there isn't much to tell about him since he is also the quietest. There is nothing that can prevent lycanthropy though scientists now acknowledge it to be real and are frantically searching for a cure. Before vampires and shape-shifters came out, the shape-shifters lived rather isolated lives. They had their group but had nobody else.

Some vampire kings that have an animal to call have ruthlessly ordered people infected since they gain power in numbers. Some have had humans infected for revenge or punishment. I was fortunate that Renaldo didn't have an animal to call in Chicago or I imagine I'd be carrying a strain myself.

Either way the options for were-animals has not been very many.

Chapter 33

By the time the third week passed, I was going completely bonkers and raging when Peter uttered one of his few words. "No."

The no was in response to my desire to go outside. To go to the store and to horrors of all horrors, do my OWN shopping. He wouldn't explain. He simply said no and I rather suspected that if I tried to leave he would forcibly keep me and I had the sinking feeling that if I called the cops, I wouldn't get much backup from then either.

I was annoyed so that when the doorbell rang I managed to beat Matthew to opening it and felt a great wave of annoyance since Jared stood there as if he didn't have a care in the world. He hadn't been forced to be cooped up for weeks presumably under doctor orders and for my own protection.

"You!"

An eyebrow arched up and he calmly said, "Yes, I'd rather hate for it to be other than me."

"He," I pointed over to Peter, "is keeping me prisoner here!"

Okay I was exaggerating a bit but not by much. "In what way?" Jared responded.

I counted to ten like I was taught to even if it was very rapidly. "In the way that I am not allowed to leave the townhouse. What other way is there?!?" I exploded anyway. Oh well. I have red hair. He should have been warned. I was capable of taking care of myself. Hell, I've acted as an executioner and let me tell you, every last one that I executed really didn't want to die and was very hard to kill. It certainly wasn't a strapped down on the gurney with a needle inserted execution.

"Ah. That was only for the first day or two because of doctors' orders. But those orders ended."

Peter had the good grace to look ashamed of himself. Though he muttered, "That's not what I was told." I heard the phrase very clearly which means Jared must have heard it too but chose to ignore it.

"Since I am here, Cassandra, would you like to go out? I'll take you to wherever you want to go."

I wanted to say nowhere with him but had a feeling that Peter had been following orders to the letter and Jared smoothly played a very fast game of cover his ass.

"Yes! Give me a minute. I need to get my weapons."

It took a little longer to strap my knives on but once they were in place all I had to do was grab my purse.

Chapter 34

Ultimately, I went to the mundane grocery store. I debated on milking it for all it was worth and have him cart me around on a epic shopping trip but decided against it. I was crawling into bed completely exhausted and sleeping, no pun intended, like the dead as it was.

It's amazing, the simple things that you can enjoy. I enjoyed shopping for my own groceries but then I'm a little weird. I've always found an immense satisfaction in going to the store and picking out an assortment of fresh produce and make selections off nicely stocked shelves. I completely appreciated the farmers that grew the food but I for one never gained satisfaction from the garden my Grandmother grew which translated into me doing the majority of the work.

So while I have been caught some years growing tomatoes in buckets in my apartment, my preferred method of harvesting food are the cool pristine and glittering aisles of the supermarket.

Jared on the other hand found the whole shopping experience amusing but I guess he would since he had a liquid diet though he was more unique than other vampires. He talked about food like it was something he had yesterday when he hadn't truly eaten a real meal in thousands of years. Which led to the one question that nobody ever seemed to ask.

"What does happen if you were eat human food?"

"We shrivel up and die." He said dead pan and I bought it until I saw the corner of his mouth twitch.

"Bastard," I muttered.

"You're fond of calling me that. It's like a human body would react if it were invaded by a foreign substance. My body rejects it.

It's not really pleasant and depending on the instance it is downright painful. However, to maintain survival so that I am not suspected I have eaten human food in the past. We all have at some point."

Periodically someone would recognize Jared and rush up to get his autograph. I was utterly ignored which was good. He'd smile apologetically to me each time but really, I understood. A couple of times old couples would frown at us disapproving.

I couldn't help but think how all of this looked to them. Not just me and Jared but vampires in general. They lived in a world that got turned upside down.

"What are you thinking about?"

"Just thinking about how the older generations have had their world turned completely upside down by vampires. They lost everything they knew."

"When we went into hiding it was to be forever, you know."

"What changed?"

"Humanity. Each decade it was harder and harder to stay hidden. Sooner or later with technology we would have been revealed and to what? Would we be used as guinea pigs in labs or could we take our place in society? We chose a fate that we might have some control over than one that we had no control over. By the time the 80's came around we felt that it was the decade to come out. We would never have found a better one."

"Grandmama always knew you were out there. She was unsurprised. Nothing surprised me. She even once wondered if the fey would jump on board but she doubted it because the fey tend to be snobbish."

"I rather would like to have met her."

"She was remarkable. She was old when she took me under her wings. She had no business raising a child but she taught me everything I knew."

"Did she tell you how she gained her knowledge?"

"Yes. It passed through generations of our family. Sometimes it skipped generations. My father and his mother are prime examples of that. He was never trained. He always rejected the stories as hocus pocus. It took my great-grandmother to teach me."

Check out was business as usual though the cashier kept looking over at Jared with a nervous look. Almost as if he would jump over, grab her, and drain her dry. I was exhausted by the time we got to the car and when offered dinner I said that I was going to order take out.

There are some days that are pizza nights and this was so one of them. Jared gave me a skeptical look but I didn't care. He started the car and I closed my eyes.

Chapter 35

When my eyes opened I was surrounded by darkness, musk, and lavender. I moved a little but realized that I was moving against someone.

"If ye keep moving like that lass, I might forget that I am a gentleman."

I gasped with surprise and realized his arms were around me but mine where around him.

"What the hell are you doing in my bed?"

"Not my idea actually. I have an ancient master vampire to hunt, remember? You fell asleep in the car and when I picked you up to carry you in, your arms wrapped themselves around me and wouldna let go. So here I am. There are witnesses if you don't believe me."

"Biased witnesses," I muttered.

"You're beautiful when you sleep."

"Flattery won't get you anywhere."

"Good because I'm not lying to you. Why didn't you tell me that you still got tired easily?"

"Would you have let me go out?"

"I wouldn't have liked it." He said shortly.

"Exactly. That's why, and I needed to get out of the place."

I moved to push myself away and suddenly I was on my back pinned by him.

"I told you lass if you moved like that again I might forget that I am a gentleman."

His mouth was so close that I couldn't help but close my eyes in anticipation. "Do you want me to kiss you lass?" My eyes flew open and uttered, "No!" more sharply than I intended. Suddenly his weight was off me. He paced back and forth for a minute before he stopped and looked at me. "One of these days, Cassandra, you need to ask yourself why when you are awake you say no but when you are unconscious or asleep, your body clings to me."

I flushed but not with anger but embarrassment because he was right. Obviously, I had no issues in trusting him when I wasn't making the decisions. He was framed by the light of the door.

"I'll leave instructions to the guards to take you out whenever you want." And he walked away and all I could do was concentrate on bringing my heart beat and breath back into order. I heard the door slam shut and I didn't have to go in the living room to know that he was gone.

Chapter 36

When I got the courage to walk into the living room it was Peter lounging around.

He looked at me with meaning. "There's some pizza in the kitchen. You sure do know how to bring out the worst in Jared."

"What's that supposed to mean?"

"Nothing." He said innocently.

"Whatever. Did he say where he was going?"

"No. Hunting probably. He's been looking for that ancient dude for some time. I doubt he'll be back here anytime soon."

"Fine by me," I grumbled.

"He's been looking for him since that night."

Matthew came stamping in, took one look at me and said, "Jeez! What happened between you to? Jared is in a right bad mood."

"Why do you assume I had anything to do with it." I shot back angrily.

"Because you usually do."

I wasn't sure how to reply to that so I just dropped the subject.

Peter was wrong about Jared giving wide berth to me. He stopped by every few days to get me out. Apparently, I wasn't allowed to leave without a supernatural bodyguard. It seemed that everyone was fine with it except me but my vote didn't count in the least.

"You know," I finally said one evening to Peter, "I've been known to execute a few vampires in my day."

"Well, you seem to have a trend in getting hurt here."

"I hardly think those are situations that one could anticipate. Being shot and stabbed by humans really don't count."

"True."

"It's not going to a change thing though is it?"

"Nope."

"That's not very fair."

"Life isn't very fair. You'll get over it."

Things had been tense ever since the night he stormed out and I seemed to be very sensitive to it. Tonight we were at the Endless Night. Jared was showing me the main areas which were finished. "You've been quiet tonight, lass."

Lass had been the compromise for Lassie. I didn't like it but if he wasn't going to compromise on just using my name, I could live with lass.

"I've been thinking about that night a little bit ago. Your still angry with me."

"Frustrated, lass. Not angry."

"Well it feels like anger from my position."

"I'm frustrated because I want to behave like a raving barbarian. I want to throw caution to the wind and seduce you. The worst part is that you won't let me. You had more than enough of my blood for me to know that. We're connected, Cassandra lass and as long as your own sense of moral ethics is involved there is nothing I can do about it until you give me leave. However, if you were honest with yourself, your moral code has nothing to do about neutrality as it is about not getting hurt."

"If I let you start kissing me, it will become more."

"Not if you don't wish it."

"That's the problem, Jared. I won't want to stop at kissing. It is easier to stop something that has never began than when something has started."

"I didna take you to be a coward, Cassandra James." He said quietly and calmly. Which just made it worse. It cut deeply as he intended because he was right. He walked off and Peter came out, "I'm to take you home when you're ready." I nodded afraid to speak over the lump that had formed in my throat. My eyes stung and I blinked rapidly to keep tears back.

Suddenly everything that I had dealt with over the years overwhelmed me and I lost it. I cried for the multitude of injuries I had healed, the lack of not having a home for years, the death of my great-grandmother, and the overwhelming loneliness that had plagued me my entire life. The loneliness was like a hungry void that threatened to swallow me whole. I feared of losing myself in it because if I did I would lose myself. And yet I feared losing myself with Jared too because he would not take bits of me, he would demand it all and what if he rejected it?

I heard panicked shouts for Jared who picked me up which just made me cry harder. "I forget lass that you are young and have been through so much for your short years. We'll figure this thing between us out eventually, I promise."

Chapter 37

The leaves were turning into a spectacular autumn and Samhain was starting to approach. I could feel the veil start thinning. Nobody said anything about my embarrassing display of female emotions, not even Jared.

There was something about Autumn that I loved. The birth of Spring is beautiful, Summer is Majestic, Winter was a bit sorrowful… but Autumn was the beautiful death where everything is harvested and even though winter would come it promised that there would a spring.

Maybe it doesn't make sense but that's how I feel. Detective Anderson called and checked in periodically. The good news is that there were no new murders. The bad news was that all leads had dried completely up. The D.A. was having fits over it and wondering what I was being paid for.

Jared was gearing up for the opening of the Endless Nights but his entire focus was consumed by finding the ancient. I personally felt that when he is found it will be when he felt like being found. He was planning but so far it felt so anticlimactic. The waiting didn't help my mood though I was no longer tired and was back to a regular training schedule.

I had just gotten home when my cell phone began to ring. "Hello?"

"Hello Cassandra. Fancy that you would pick up." Detective Anderson said. He voice sounded slightly strained and a bit odd. Something was not right.

"Are you alright?"

"Yes. I'm fine for now."

"You don't sound fine."

"I know."

"Who else is there?"

"He has me Cassandra. Dear God he has me!," he choked off with a scream of agonizing pain.

"Mike Anderson! What's happening!" I screamed into the phone.

"He really shouldn't have done that," a dry heavily accented voice said.

"What did you do to him?"

"Oh nothing permanent. At least for now. I'm actually surprised he really called you. I didn't think he'd do it."

"Where is he?"

"I'm going to give you an address outside the city. Do you have pen and paper?"

"Yes."

"Then take this down."

I hastily scribbled the very specific directions that he was giving me.

"You are to come alone, Ms. James. And if you don't it'll just be more people to kill and it will be all your fault. I don't think you want that, do you?"

"No I wouldn't. What will happen if I don't bother to come?"

The voice laughed. "You really do like to push the envelope don't you? If you do not come alone, you will find your friend, one piece at a time. I will tear him apart piece by piece starting with fingers and toes. Be here by midnight. Your little friend will not be harmed if you come."

I ran into the living room, "Where is Jared?"

"He's down for the night. Cassandra, you're scaring me. What's wrong."

"Shit? For how much longer will he be down?"

"Possibly for several more hours."

"Our ancient vampire just called. He has Detective Anderson and we are going to have to get him back."

"We need to wait for Jared to wake up"

"We can't afford to wait. He said if I didn't come he would kill Detective Anderson. And not just the easy death. He said he would start pulling him apart piece by piece starting with his fingers and toes. Detective Anderson isn't like me. He can't even possibly hope to survive physically or mentally something like that."

"This is what we'll do. We'll form a team to go in." Matthew began reasonably.

I started to protest that I had to go alone but he put his finger up and said, "Hear me out."

"This place you're going to go to takes you by the Endless Night. So let's rendezvous there and I'll have a team waiting for us to go hunting. If Jared is awake he gets to come with us. If he doesn't, we'll tell him all about it when he does wake up."

It sounded reasonable but I didn't want to be responsible for any of Jared's peoples deaths but at the same time I knew this was a trap specifically for me. It would be time consuming to make a plan but reasonable. When I nodded my agreement Matthew relaxed visibly and I went to my bedroom to get my execution outfit on. I'd discovered a long time ago that I wanted to wear black which didn't show unfortunate stains. When I strapped the last weapon on which was a sword that I had custom made, I caught a glimpse of myself in the mirror and couldn't help but think that I looked like a warrior princess somehow. When I walked out, I must not have been the only one because Matthew let out a low whistle of approval.

Chapter 38

When we arrived at the Endless Nights, we drove into a huge garage and met up with a group of others. I had written a message for Jared on the way there. I was amazed really on how organized everyone and their willingness to be involved. I finally asked why.

"Jared told us that when he is down to follow you as if he was the one giving the orders." A perky girl with bubble gum pink hair said offhandedly without even looking up from a map that she had spread out on a table. "Of course this is a trap but maybe we'll get lucky. Personally, if we can end this I'll be happy. I'm getting tired of hunting the bastard."

"Well of course it is a trap. I'd rather not spring the trap but then I don't want anything to happen to Detective Anderson because he doesn't deserve a gruesome death."

I was getting impatient to be back on the road and the girl noticed my impatience.

"My name is Naomi and I know you want to be on the road. However, this vampire, he wants you to rush without thinking. Rushing can lead to necessary deaths, ma'am. Plus I really don't want to explain to Jared why I let you run head long into danger when you get yourself killed. So let's take an hour to make some plans. You have time to get there and I know old vampires. They have a code of rules that even if they are evil and sadistic are their rules and they play by them."

I hated it when people were right and she was right.

"Fine." I said shortly.

She flashed me a smile. "Don't you just hate it when people are right?" And I couldn't help but smile back. I liked her. The way she gave orders was surprising since I wasn't expecting to see it in her. She was very petite in compared to the hulking men around her.

"Surprising isn't it?" Peter said quietly.

"What is?"

"Her. But don't make any mistakes with her. She is bright, bubbly, and excessively happy. She's also the pride alpha and viciously deadly."

I don't surprise very often but in a pride makeup the alpha usually is a male. Even among the cats even when the female in nature is the dominant. It was rare for an alpha to be female.

"Does she get challenged often?"

"Nope. Everyone is afraid of her and she's not a tyrant. But even if she was, it wouldn't matter."

"She's that good?"

"That good and better." And I noted a tone of pride in him and looked over.

"Is she mated?"

"No?"

"You like her." And I watched with interest as the big man slowly flushed.

"Don't say anything, please? I'm not a leader and she deserves another leader as her mate so it's completely impossible."

"Suit yourself but I think you're doing yourself a disservice and maybe her as well."

"Just leave it be." He whispered and casually walked away.

Chapter 39

Even though I felt a great deal of impatience, I had to admit that I was sitting shotgun in an SUV within the hour with a small army near me. I had plenty of time and Jared was still not awake which had me pacing back and forth biting my nails, literally. Naomi bit her lower lip hard in indecision before she finally said we were ready. Admittedly, I was going in with a small army of highly trained shape shifters.

When sitting in the SUV, I was introduced to John (who grinned when I said, ah there is John), Michael, and DeRon. John immediately impressed me as a happy go-lucky guy with a perpetual sense of humor. He had spiky blond hair and impressed me as being someone who should be on a beach somewhere with a surf board. DeRon had skin so dark that the word midnight came to mind and had a Jamaican accent. He was the type to give himself a pep talk to get him ready. Michael was another quiet type and had an uncanny resemblance to Matthew but no relation when I asked.
.

I was nervous. I had my own self-doubts naturally. I recognized that there was a very good chance I wouldn't survive this but I pushed those doubts to the back and sealed them off because it did me no good. I had to be confident. The plan was to send me in as bait and then everyone rush the vampire when he made an appearance with the hope that someone would get lucky. He might be a badass but even badasses can lose if attacked by enough people at one time.

I was staring unseeingly as the lights of the city flashed by until the lights were fewer and fewer in-between. That is when Naomi started speaking.

"I want to go over the plan again before we get there. This thing wants Cassandra rather badly. So we'll dangle her out there like the juiciest bait ever. The place we're going to used to be a prominent factory but has since become dilapidated and abandoned. It was used for a while as a warehouse so you might encounter empty pallets. She'll walk in first and then we'll be not far behind her. Does that sound good to you Cassandra?"

"Sounds fine to me."

We made a few more turns and you could see the building. It was enormous with pieces of roof missing here and there and broken windows. There were several no trespassing signs that had graffiti spray painted on them.

What used to be a parking lot was losing its battle to mother nature and had weeds growing out of it. It looked like a set to a horror film and I was the main cast. I attached a flashlight to my belt and carried my sword in one hand. The SUV was positioned so that when I opened the double doors to the factory the light would shine in.

I allowed myself to be aware of everything but search as I might, I couldn't feel any preternatural presence except for what I brought with me. I walked slowly and carefully to the double doors. It seemed like forever before I reached the doors and when I did so, I took my other hand to push them open. I wasn't about to let go of my sword.

I used my leg to kick the doors wide open after I turned the latch. They creaked with age as they swung open and the light from the headlights bounced off the swirls of stirred up dust. As I learned to see through it all I noticed there was a chair in direct line of sight with someone in. It took me a few minutes but I realized it was Detective Anderson tied to it. I resisted the impulse to run to him but carefully continued in.

As I approached I could see that he was gagged and trembling. When I reached him I signaled for the rest to come into the room so that even if I went down he would be guaranteed to save.

When I reached Anderson he kept shaking his head wildly back and forth. I removed his gag. "It's a trap." Was the first words out of his mouth.

"Of course it's a trap. And I am here to spring it."

"There's nothing here, Cassandra. He's afraid of you. He said that when he was a boy that an aura told his mother that a red head girl would be his end. He's going somewhere else. He used me as a decoy."

"Then it was rather stupid of him to mess with me then wasn't it? Where's he going?"

"I have no idea. But he wants Jared dead. I do know that. He wasn't much of a talker which is unusual. Most psychopaths just love to talk about themselves and their conquests. Especially the ones who aren't afraid of being caught or have been caught and have nothing to lose. But he is freaky that one. I thought I was as good as dead."

"Did he hurt you?"

"Nothing out of the ordinary. Hit me in the head to subdue me and then tied me up. But he was careful not to kill me."

Detective Anderson was stretching as he stood up from being released and soon fell down.

"How long have you been like this?"

"Since last night. He was waiting for me at my home. I wasn't sure if you would come."

"Well of course I would. We're partners, aren't we?" Detective Anderson flashed me a look of profound gratitude because he didn't really know me or I him all that well. I could have easily written him off. I even knew a few who would have which is the unfortunate truth. I just wasn't built like them though and believed I was the better for it.

Chapter 40

John and Michael helped prop Detective Anderson up as he transported to the SUV. When we arrived, Michael looked over at me, "So where to next?"

I bit my lip hard with indecision, "I guess back to the Endless Night."

As we were pulling out from the parking lot collectively, someone suddenly landed in the road in front of us. Michael hits his breaks so hard that we all leaned forward and then pushed back into our seats. Detective Anderson grunted in pain. It took me a minute to realize that it was Jared.

Furiously, I jumped out. "Are you crazy?!" I shriek. "You could have gotten us all killed just now!"

"Me? I'm not the one who decided to go recklessly into an unknown place in the middle of the night! You endangered yourself and others!" He shouted back.

"I had it under control!"

"You had it under control because he LET you have it under control, Cassandra. IF he is older than me, he didn't survive the past millenniums by being stupid. He survived by being clever and proving that he was useful to some purpose or another!"

"He had Detective Anderson. What was to do? Leave him to die?!?"

"Yes! That was exactly what you should have done. You should have waited until I was awake."

Detective Anderson spoke up, "Well personally, I am rather grateful that Cassandra chose to come after me."

"See!" I said. "I did the right thing by coming after him. He is my partner when it comes to preternatural crime!"

"You were being foolish to rush in and you could have endangered my people!"

"FINE! I didn't want to bring your people in the first place! I'll never involve them on anything ever again!"

"That was not what I meant!" Jared said frustrated.

"That's bullshit Jared. Say what you mean or not at all. I'm not going to play the what-does-his-highness-feel-today game."

"Cassandra, I hate to say this, but you two sound like an old married couple." Detective Anderson injected grinning.

"Shut up!" Jared and I said in unison.

My cell phone began to ring.

Annoyed I answered, "What do you want?"

"Temper, temper." The dry heavily accented voice said with what I swore was a bit of amusement. "I didn't interrupt a lover's quarrel did I?" Without thinking of exactly who it was, I snapped out, "Don't be absurd." Jared was making what appeared to be chocking noises.

For a second I thought my heart had stopped for a beat when I realized who it was that I had just spoken to in a very flippant manner. I must have gone pale because even Jared got still.

"So it was a trap?" I asked trying to inject the same flippant tone.

"Trap has such a nasty sound to it. I look at it as more of a test."

"Don't you think you're old enough not to be playing such games?" Jared was making frantic motions and I turned my back. "So what test have you set me up with next?"

"It's been rumored that you are naturally suspicious. I gather it's true?"

"Of course it's true. Again…you wouldn't be calling me to discuss the weather. Unless you're a moron of course. Is it possible to live so long and be as dumb as a post?" Even Detective Anderson was waving frantically.

"You're to meet me on the roof of the mall and we're going to fight."

"And if I have something better to do?" I asked injecting enough dare in my tone as I possibly could.

"I will slaughter everyone inside."

"If you can get inside. Which I highly doubt."

"That sure of yourself?" No I wasn't really but I wouldn't let him know that.

"Of course but if you insist. I hope you don't take too long to die."

"Be here. At the appropriate time of course."

"How long do we have to get there? If I decide to get there that is."

"One hour. I must say, I admire how calm you are taking your impending death."

"Who says I'm going to die?"

"You'll die. But if you want to comfort yourself with the delusion. Suit yourself. You now have 59 minutes." He hung up and I looked over at Jared.

"You caught all of this?"

He nodded. "Most unfortunately. If you're going to do something like that, try to warn me! I recognize who it is too."

"And?"

"He wasn't a fan of our coming out but he abstained in the vote. He left the process and nobody ever heard another word. We figured he had gone somewhere remote like Siberia. His current name is Ivan."

"Is he good?"

"One of the best fighters I've ever known and very old. Honestly, he's so old that he's not sure if he came from the Steppes of Russia or not. He's forgotten a large part of his human life."

"Can you fly us both?"

"No. I will fly myself and you will stay as far away."

"Actually," I argued. "He wants us both there."

"He's had disappointment in his life. He can live with this one."

"I'm coming with you."

"NO, you are not." Jared said firmly again.

"I will come whether you fly me there or not. I'll follow because he has made a condition. He wants me there. So your choices are take me with you, or have me follow behind. But either way, I will be there on that rooftop in fifty-four minutes."

Jared paced a bit swearing, or at least I thought it was. I wasn't sure of the language. He grabbed me and we were up in the air before I could blink.

Chapter 41

He had grabbed me and took me up in the air so quickly, I was feeling distinctly unsecure because I couldn't get a good enough grip and I refused to let myself relax.

"Relax Lass, I haven't ever dropped someone in the air." He murmured.

Which I silently thought was easy for him to say. He was the one that could fly and he was the one who if he did fall, would be able to get back up.

"Stay out of this fight. If you have to save yourself, fight, but let me take care of this one."

I opened my mouth to protest some and he angrily said, "No buts! I don't want your death on my hands. For some reason you are dear to me. ."

And that shut me up. I was dear to him? "I'm dear to you?"

"Of course. Gods only know why. You're a real pain in the ass sometimes."

Naturally, I vowed to be involved. But dear to him? It was just too complicated for it all to be possible and for some reason that thought saddened me greatly. Fortunately, I didn't have long to dwell on it because I saw the Endless Nights glittering ahead as the first drops of rain began to fall and a rumble of thunder crashed into the night sky.

Awesome! We were going to have a thunderstorm and the one thing you don't want is to be the tallest thing in the sky for lightening.

Chapter 42

Jared descended into some woods instead of going straight to the Endless Night which surprised me greatly.

"Walk the flying off so that if you have to fight as soon as we land you will have your legs instantly. How much time do we have?"

I looked at my cell phone clock. "Twenty minutes."

"I have time to start evacuating The Endless Nights." He said quietly.

"I don't think that's a good idea. He would expect to see people coming out the front door."

Jared smiled wickedly. "But that's why I have a back door."

"What do you mean?"

"Cassandra, I've survived through all sorts of political and religious upheaval. Do you really think that I would come to this country and not assume that sooner or later it would fall? It's always important for a place to have a few backdoors. Just in case."

"And wouldn't you expect to find that he would have some guesses what they are and would be waiting for them?"

"No. I personally built some of them so that I and I alone know where they are and where they lead to. Then there are the ones that were built but nobody realizes what I had done."

"How?"

"I used over 50 different contractors and none of them suspected a thing. People don't build escape routes like they used to."

"Fine…have it your way. It's your call but I think it is a bad idea in this case. He isn't interested in your people. He's interested in you and for some reason, me."

"You're right. That makes sense."

He picked me up again and we were up in the air. As soon as we were up my hip was starting to like it was on fire.

"He's so definitely there." I gasped as the pain spread and I felt like I was completely on fire.

"How do you know?"

"I'm hurting."

"I don't feel a thing."

"Lucky you. Are you sure you can fight him?"

"I'm a match for him you know when it comes to fighting skills. Cassandra my dear, there are only so many ways to kill a man and he was a man at some point."

"If you sever his head, make sure the head does not see the body. Keep it out of sight of the rest of him."

"Isn't that a little excessive?"

"Just do it," I said breathlessly. Jesus I hurt. I gripped my sword as if my life depended upon it.

"You're in agony, lass, Please just let me put you down outside."

"Don't you dare!" I gasped. "I don't want to crawl up to that damn roof top."

"Suit yourself. Try not to get yourself killed."

He landed and I fell down to the ground as if a million knives were stabbing me. The pain was all over and seemed to radiate from within me and I vomited most inelegantly which somehow seemed to make it all the worst. I felt Jared hesitate and I hissed not to though the pain was unbearable. He couldn't be distracted by anything. Least of all by me.

I heard the sound of a slow clap and I looked in the direction that it was coming from.

"Brava! Brava!" Came the familiar accented voice which made me grip my sword tighter and I managed to pull myself up to a standing position.

"What do you want, Ivan?" Jared asked.

"Her. You. And a return of anonymity that will never happen."

"You could have voted no. You chose to abstain."

"What is the point of a vote if it is meaningless? The decision for us to return back in the open was a done decision and whether I voted yes or no would not have mattered."

"Again… even though vampires did come out in the open didn't mean you had to. You could have continued to hide if you want."

"Possibly though I was instantly suspected as being one and in Russia, vampires are not treated so well. So I have come to America to wreak my vengeance."

"I accept that you hold me responsible. But what on earth does Cassandra have to do with this?"

He laughed with derision.

"You don't know?" I saw a flash of doubt and confusion flash instantly across Jared's face and bit my lip in worry.

"Evidently," Jared said flatly.

"Ah well. I won't tell you since it doesn't really matter." He looked around.

"I must say, Jared, you did well with this. The human race have come up with marvelous abilities in building. Pity that it will not fulfill its purpose."

"Oh I rather think I will win this battle." Jared said simply.

"Suit yourself in your delusions."

"Are you sure you aren't the one that's not deluded?" I asked. My vision was rimmed in black as I fought to remain conscious. I could see lips moving but lost my ability to hear. The vampire made a few steps towards before I saw Jared draw his sword and the next sound I heard was the crash of steel hitting steel.

I fought to remember who I was and what I was doing there despite the fire of pain searing me alive. Even though I had previously seen Jared spar this was a different type of fighting that I saw out of him. This was the fighting of a warrior who was battling for victory and to live. I could honestly not tell who was better. Then suddenly I saw one shooting up in the sky. It took me a split second to realize that it was Jared.

And as suddenly as he was airborne, you was falling to the ground writhing in agony. I winced when I heard the thud of his form hitting the ground. That's when it hit me that Ivan wasn't so old that his existence made your bones hurt. It was his own personal ability and that was my department though I flinched at the thought of opening myself up to more pain.

In fact, I worried that it wouldn't make me pass out which would do Jared absolutely no good, but I had to do something because I knew that if Jared died, that I would be next.

I closed my eyes for them to fly open when I heard a groan and saw that Jared had been wounded. I willed that I drop all of my shields. I flinched physically from the pain but I had to do it. Jared was back on his feet and fighting again though I knew he was bleeding.

The pain for me was getting steady less as I embraced it to make it mine. I'd borrowed abilities before but nothing like this. But then I'd never encountered a vampire that had his ability before. I felt amazingly strong and just a little drunk on it.

Jared was suddenly back on the ground and Ivan was standing over him and I realized the next blow would be the death blow.

"Coward!" I shouted.

Ivan stopped and turned his head to me. Jared was laying on the ground writhing in pain from his injury. "Cassandra, no! Don't" he calls out.

"I, a coward?" The vampire said incredulously.

I shrugged and figured if in for a penny, in for a pound. "Yes! You are a vile coward of the worst order! You want to mold away like some mummy rather than face a new world. You are a coward."

"I am no coward! Little girl you have no idea the wars I've fought!"

"So? Bravery on the battlefield isn't anything." I said flippantly because I knew it would irritate. I didn't believe it because I respected our American warriors but it wasn't about what I believed. It was about killing the bastard in any form that I could."

"It's everyday life that you have to not tuck tail and run from." I got my first clear look at him. He wasn't ugly. Just very non-descript with black hair. He wasn't very tall. Jared towered over him but when he was made he probably was average height. Humans were smaller back then. Jared would have been considered a giant then. There was something a little off in his features that made him a little alien looking but I couldn't put my finger on it and he still looked human. There was no question about it. He would have been able to fit in with an open society if he been willing to adapt.

His lips thinned and his nostrils flared a bit so I knew that I was hitting a nerve. "You're going to die tonight."

"Whether I die is yet to be seen."

"You can't possibly be a match to me, girl." Yet there was a slight crease that indicated he wasn't one hundred percent positive of his statements which I found intriguing.

"Oh I disagree. I am too a match. I'm standing up aren't I?"

The crease deepened. So I continued because I knew just as well that he should be able to break me in a split second. But if I could throw him off balance well I might come out of this one alive and that was just fine with me.

"You know what I think? I think this whole production is because you are emasculated somehow and you don't want the world to find out about your lack of manhood." His nostrils flared again. Point for me! Jared was yelling for me to shut the fuck up.

"You know you should listen to Jared girl. Perhaps, I just liked things the way they were but Jared made a decision for all of us whether we wanted it or not." His voice was a little shrill from the anger that I was goading him into.

"Not so. It was voted by the vampire committee to go public. You could have had a vote," Jared said pulling himself up.

"My vote was a minority as you well know. To many of you young ones wanted to come back out of the shadows of myth where we should have remained."

"So you think you're a monster and should be treated like a monster?" I asked.

"Exactly. And I will prove my monstrosity on your body."

I smiled. "You can try. You won't be very successful but there are always points for trying."

"Bitch! You deserve to die just for your arrogant mouth."

"I know. It's been a failing of mine." And I did the one thing I probably shouldn't have since I wasn't 100 percent sure on how to do what I was about to do. I buffed my finger nails against my shirt and examined them as if he was inconsequential. I felt his rage flare and heard Jared groan.

He rushed towards me but Jared was there to stop him so he had to turn and strike at Jared. Sparks flew from metal on metal. This time I was able to follow the fight and was impressed with the mastery of a true fight to the death. If it wasn't one that was intended to end with the death of another it would be almost beautiful. Jared had the advantage of his height but his opponent seemed to be a little faster.

I saw Jared fly towards a tree and hit it. The trunk cracked and he wasn't getting back up. Ivan was about to strike the death blow again and all the pain that I managed to absorb without thinking I released it all. I knew I had struck home when I heard him hiss.

I had to give him a great deal of credit. He didn't fall down but he looked at me astonished. "You really don't like having a dose of your own medicine tossed at you, do you?" He said "You!" and a look of mixed recognition and I didn't have much time to register confusion because he rushed me. I managed to block the blow, that should have killed me, just in time but even I had to admit it was just in time. He on the other hand was furious and swung again and again. It felt like he was trying to beat me down into the ground and he was succeeding.

I knew the pain thing was a weapon for him and I kept pushing the power but it seemed to not be affecting him much to my frustration, and the fact that I kept fighting back was frustrating to him. He was trying to kill me in earnest.

"I killed you once. I'll do it again."

"You have to be delusional," I grunted as I blocked another blow. My arms were aching and I wouldn't be able to continue for too much longer. I hoped to hell Jared would help me finish him.

"Oh I recognize you, witch. You came back just to die at my hands all over again."

He struck again and again at this point. I kept waiting for Jared to get it together and finish him off and I was getting very tired. If this kept going on I was going to end up making a fatal mistake and I simply was not ready to die yet.

Then inexplicably I got lucky and sliced the vampire once with my sword but it wasn't very big. He was holding his wound like I had opened him up completely though. He brought his full will down on me and I collapsed in pain again and was dry heaving since I didn't have anything left in my stomach. The world was going dark at the edges again and knew if I didn't get it together I was dead.

As I heaved again I thought to bad vampires couldn't vomit and a little voice in my head asked "why not?" Why not indeed. He seemed to enjoy watching me do it. So I pushed with all my might the thought. I saw his eyes widen for a split second before suddenly a spray of blood came out of his mouth. Unfortunately, I got hit with it and I closed my eyes reflectively to protect my eyes and tried not to just cringe.

I felt another spray hit me and then a thud. I felt a hand touch me and I reacted but Jared said "It's just me. It's over." I stood as he wiped my face with a handkerchief and he embraced me. "You were spectacular, lassie. You saved my life and will forever be honored in this city."

I wiped the blood from my eyes so that I could see. After a moment I looked over at the remains and saw the body crawling blindly towards the head. I grabbed the hilt of my knife from my boot and crawled over to the bleeding stump of the almost dead vampire. I took my knife and stuck it in his chest. The body twitched. Then I slowly carved the heart out of the body.

"We need to quarter the body. Burn each piece including the head in separate fires. Keep the ashes from mixing and dispose of the ashes in separate bodies of water."

"Isn't that a little excessive?" Jared queried?

"He was crawling towards his severed head. Doesn't that call for a bit of excess or let me put it like this, do you want to fight him again?"

"Not really."

"Then let's make sure he doesn't come back."

Chapter 43

I was tired and filthy. All I wanted to do was get on with the disposal of the damn body, get clean, and get some rest. Unfortunately, my name was mud in the press and I looked massively incompetent.

So I reluctantly said, "We need to call the police and the press. They need to see that this was a real matter and not smoke and mirrors."

"If you think you're up to it. I'll arrange for a copy of the surveillance footage to be given too."

The media beat the police department to the scene. Detective Anderson was in a wheel chair and confirmed that this was the vampire who made confession of his deeds to the innocents. The chief of police ruled it a legal execution based on preliminary statements but assured the public he would review the footage just to make sure.

It was nearing dawn when the ashes were gathered in bags. I was sticky from the dry blood and I wasn't sure if I was ever going to get clean again. Jared came up with the brilliant idea of dousing the flames with holy water mixed with silver nitrate. He handed each bag to one of his guards on motorcycles with instructions to go on road trips. I don't know what bodies of water the ashes were dumped in and I didn't care. As long as they never met each other.

I wanted to go home and bathe but Jared insisted on using his baths and for once I was grateful. It took three changes of the tub water and a copious amount of scrubbing but I was clean and barely registered the drive home in the limo or him carrying me to my lavender sheets.

"Cassandra?"

"Hmm?"

"Thank ye, my wee lass."

I wanted to retort that I wasn't his wee lass but decided not to fight the point just then. So I said, "Your welcome" with as much grace as possible. He pressed his lips on me and before I could kiss him back he was gone.

I was out before he could close the door softly behind him.

Chapter 44

I became the darling of the media all over again which was a little embarrassing, considering how much they maligned me. But I always knew the media was a fickle lover. The footage from the night heavily edited was played over and over again. But after a while things settled down.

Detective Anderson healed quickly from his injuries and the DA ruled that I carried out a legal execution which was a relief since he was still very unhappy with me not cooperating when it came to my father.

My father went back to California and made no attempt to contact me. Though much to my surprise my mother filed for divorce citing irreconcilable differences. I was surprised even more when my phone rang and she requested a meeting.

I don't know how that will go but I guess I'm game. My life was back on track and everything had settled down to a normal routine. We were having an exceptionally harsh winter brewing this year. The Mall of Endless Nights announced a grand opening at the start of December. The date would be December 31st.

I received a personal invitation to attend which I had tucked into a drawer without replying to. Jared and I had not spoken since that night. It was all so very complicated. I knew I had to make a decision about him. But he seemed to be giving me space. My semester now that I wasn't constantly in the hospital was going well with my students were dreading finals.

The college was impressed though concerned about my recent stints in the hospital. I had to assure them that it happened from time to time but in this case it was a 6000 year old vampire. That they didn't occur very often. Or at least I hoped not.

I dreamed of Jared every night. Everyone that was with me that night stopped and visited. Much to Peter's amazement, Naomi came up to him a few days later and told him that she had just about enough of the nonsense and they were officially a couple. I never dreamed again of my Grandmother. I rather suspected she had moved on and this was the last I would hear from her.

I opened the pages of Little Women, a book I had always wanted to read but never seemed to have time for. "Christmas won't be Christmas without any presents," grumbled Jo, lying on the rug.

Author's Note:

Thank you so much for reading my book. I greatly appreciate the time you have taken. When building my world so much back story popped up as well. Characters that didn't have a dominate voice have their own stories they want to tell. Detective Anderson and Melina for instance have their own tale that is begging to be told eventually. In my world the vampires are legal citizens now. But that was not always the case. How did the monsters get rights? The following story that I am including as a bonus tells you that tale.

There will be a second book for sure. I'm positive there will be a third. The rough draft of the second book is completed and the working title for it is called "The 100 Nights". This one starts out differently than any of the other books.

The Fight For Equality

It was a cool crisp January morning that was bitingly cold. It was one of those mornings that a person would have preferred to stay in bed. However, it was not going to happen this morning. The streets around the courthouse were barricaded with the hopes of keeping two factions separate and the police were put on high alert with preparations of dealing with a riot.

On one side were members of the Human Society and various other anti-monster coalitions. On the other side were members of the pro-monster coalitions. Each that had beliefs of their own. The anti-monster believed that they were spawn of the devil and should all be killed on site. The pro-monster members believed that vampires and confirmed shape-shifters of every flavor should have the right to live equally among everyone else.

The chants from both sides were deafening and clashed with each other. One side was shouting "Humanity First!" The other was shouting, "Equality!" It seemed like the entire country was divided and had been divided from the moment, the vampire king of Charlotte, NC came forward and shattered the existence of the world. The monsters were real. The myths were based on the terrible reality.

His name was Jared MacAllistair and until 1982 had been an eccentric recluse. Now he was on his way to federal court to present the case that monsters should have the same rights that everyone else does. This was a case that was controversial to say the least and was already widely believed to be destined for the Supreme Court because it was addressing constitutional law.

It was a controversial case because it might be the case that would change everything. There were so many questions that would be asked in this trial. The sentiment against the monsters was turning to their favor and even the ones who disliked them have been known to admit that perhaps the laws needed to be changed. That perhaps the no questions asked kill on sight policy needed to be reviewed. That is if you managed to kill one. There were so many new questions and all because of one young woman who had an unfortunate incident just six months ago.

Her name was Rachel Smith. She was nineteen years old and a college student at UNCC. It was a Friday night and had decided to meet a group of her friends at a nightclub in Winston-Salem. She had a good night out but decided to leave early. She did not return home that night. Nor did she come home the next day. Her body was found brutally murdered a week later after an intense manhunt was began. The farmer was very proud for "bagging one of them shape-shifter freaks". The problem was that she was not a shape-shifter. There was outrage because the policy had led to a string of hate crimes towards otherwise hard working citizens and likened to the Salem witch hunts.

The Rachel Smith incident inflamed the nation and parts of the world because she was merely a young woman who had gone out for a night out, got a flat in the wrong spot at the wrong time, who met the wrong person and she died as a result.

When the limo arrived at the courthouse, the crowds erupted and the police struggled to maintain the barricades that kept both sides from clashing with each other. Jared stepped out with his attorney with a cool confidence that seemed to fill the air. He was wearing a black suit that had to be tailored given his tall stature and dark sunglasses that hid his stunning blue eyes. He did not smile or make any move to acknowledge the crowds cheering and booing. He walked into the courthouse with cool ease flanked by his body guards, as if he did not hear the accusations that he was a Satan worshipper or that he was in fact the devil himself. In fact, when his head was turned away from the cameras you could catch the corners of his mouth twitching to repress a smile at the foolishness of some people.

There was something about him. A cool calmness that one could presume was either a façade if you were a friend and sheer arrogance if you were a foe. When the court went into session you could hear the roars from the crowd outside. The judge was Abigail Lewis who was noted for her impartiality and she had to be in order to survive the pre-trial motions and jury selection. This case had propelled her career several steps ahead. She was careful in all her rulings in making sure if she couldn't find it written down in law, that she wouldn't grant the motion. She even double checked the lawyers work like an unruly school teacher and was known to point out the flaws in using the law if needed.

She even looked like a school teacher with her hair pulled back in a severe bun. Her hair was a chestnut brown except for two streaks of silver on either side of her temple. She understood that no matter what the outcome for this trial, it was going to move forward towards the Supreme Court. However, she was determined to make sure all the I's got dotted and the T's got crossed.

And it all culminated down to the one moment. When the jury was lead in, the judge entered the courtroom and told everyone to be seated, and the opening arguments began. Much to the dislike of Judge Lewis, Jared did the opening arguments. While she would grudgingly admit he was brilliant and knew what he was doing, he was not a lawyer so it didn't sit too well with her for a non-attorney to do such things.

When Jared stood he turned around and addressed the jurors and courtroom.

"Ladies and Gentleman of the courtroom and jury, my name is Jared MacAllistair and I am over two thousand years old. I am also a vampire. My bodyguards who accompanied me here today can change into Leopards. I freely admit to who and what I am. I am the vampire king of Charlotte and have been since Tryon was a mere dirt road.

You will hear testimony over the next days by experts who will prove to you what I claim. There will be clergy who will discuss how creatures like me cannot possibly have souls. The latter is quite possible. Since I have never seen a soul I am not sure if I possess one. What I do know is that we love, grieve, and have the same cares and concerns about our world that you do. You will hear testimony explaining that it is better to hunt me and my shape-shifters down no matter what because we are an abomination. This is the United States of America and like it or not, we should be equal in our abilities to have a right to pursue happiness without fear of someone trying to kill us when we walk out our front door because the law says they can."

For five days each side brought their case. The government showed gruesome pictures of 'victims' of attacks by monsters, and Jared and his team countered them with images from crimes humans had perpetrated. He and his legal team challenged the accuracy of the images and brought together a very compelling case of a more human side. The biggest focus was on the shape-shifters because they began life as humans but were transformed by being victims themselves of attacks in most cases.

It was a difficult case. The jurors themselves were visibly torn by the testimony and evidence that was brought. And it all came down to the last day in which final closing arguments were delivered. The Defense argued bitterly over him delivering the closing arguments. Mostly because the defense new that Jared would completely hammer them. But the judge decided that if Jared was allowed to deliver the opening arguments then he most certainly could deliver the closing.

When Jared stood up he had everyone's attention. "It was a midsummer day when a young woman was going home from a night out with friends. Her car had a flat tire and because of the remote location she was in she could not call out on her cell phone. It was dark and lonely. With her flash light she tried to change her tire. One can speculate that she was unable to get the lug nuts to budge. Because of the time and the remoteness of her location there were no cars coming that would stop to help her. She spied in a distance a light. It belonged to Sebastian McCoy, a farmer in the area.

The young woman knocked on his door to ask for help. What opened was the devil you accuse me of being. Evidence shows he sexually assaulted her brutally. He made sure he let her go so that as she ran away he could shoot her brutally repeatedly. He openly bragged about killing one of those shape–shifters."

"Objection!" The lawyer of the defense shouted out.

"On what grounds?"

"He is using this unfortunate incident to his advantage."

"Then I am sure when it is your turn, you will come up with something compelling."

"But…"

"You are overruled. Continue Mr. MacAllistair and hurry up to the point."

"Her name was Rachel Smith and she died a senseless death. As long as these laws remain there will be instances. There will be citizens who will use the laws to their advantage. She was not one of us. She was one of you. She could have been your daughter, sister, wife, mother, aunt, niece, or friend. And she died because she said no and wanted a little help. Her murderer almost got off with his claim. If it had not been for her family having a little authority to get the forensics to look into her pathology to discover she was completely human he would have been cleared of the crime. By allowing the laws to stand as they are now you are inviting more incidents like her. Next time will it happen to someone you know? We have never gone away. We have always been here. Living and working beside you. The difference is you know that we are real and exist. So we are not this scourge that is going to take over the world and enslave humanity. That is in the mind of fiction writers. I ask only that you judge by what you think is right and fair."

It took the jury four hours to come to a verdict. The fact that they deliberated so shortly made the defense argue that they did not fully go over the facts and suggested they spend more time discussing the matter. The judge wouldn't hear of it as it was a unanimous decision. The law was ruled to be illegal and it was the first step towards making the monsters legal citizens of the United States. It took a few more years in appeals, several more incidents like what had occurred with the Rachel Smith case, and the economy nearly completely collapsing, but ultimately the Supreme Court included the monsters as citizens. However, in their wisdom they also ruled that given their demonstrated special abilities that they could be subject to swift and immediate execution by law enforcement if they were to ever misbehave.

Within hours plans for The Mall of the Endless Night were announced and our world as we knew it had suddenly changed yet again. Whether it was for the better or the worst remained to be seen.

www.ingramcontent.com/pod-product-compliance
Lightning Source LLC
Chambersburg PA
CBHW070919130626
46555CB00001B/205